EXIT SIDEWAYS

Stan Jones

Copyright © 2026 by Stan Jones

All rights reserved.

No portion of this book may be reproduced in any form without written permission from the publisher or author, except as permitted by U.S. copyright law.

Published by
Bowhead Press
Box 240264
Anchorage AK 99524

ISBN: 979-8-9943116-0-8

Chapter One

THE BEDSIDE CLOCK reads 8:13 when my phone pings and Jamie Lochner's ID pops up on the screen.

"Jamie?" I say past a sleep-furred tongue. "What did Tony—"

"He's dead!" she shrieks. "I...when I came...he was...I went into the store and I didn't see him so I called the number you gave me and it rang from behind the counter and I looked over and he was down there...the phone was ringing in the pocket of his shorts and he was...somebody shot him. Barney killed him!"

"What? He—where are you?"

"I'm parked in front of that place where Tony works...where...oh, God, what do I do now...Dana?"

"Are you sure he's dead?"

"I think...yes, I'm sure...he...he...he's lying behind the counter and his head...his head..."

"He was shot in the head?"

Jamie gets out a muffled "Yes," then breaks down in sobs.

When she stops I ask, "In the head?"

"Yes," she says, "and...and...there was a lot of blood on his chest, on his, his shirt. I think he was shot there, too, and he wasn't moving and there was...there was..."

"There was what?"

"A fly. It landed in his eye, then it crawled up his nose. Oh, Dana."

I wait out another bout of sobs.

"Did you call 911?"

"No, I, I'm scared...I can't...Barney did this and he'll...he'll..."

"How do you know your husband did it? It could have been robbery. Or maybe some kind of biker thing with that Harley you gave him."

"No, it was Barney," she says. "It was him, I know it was. And I'm going back to Texas. I have to get out of this place."

"Don't do that. Whatever you do, don't run."

"Then what do I do?"

"All right, listen, can you drive?"

"Yeah," she says. "I think so. I don't know."

"Well, calm down and come back up here to Palm Springs and meet me at Ike's office. He's your lawyer and he will, we will, we'll figure something out together, the three of us."

"I'll try, I'll..."

More sobs and another wait.

"You can do this, okay? Call me on the way if you need to, okay? I'll call Ike now and we'll start figuring this out, okay? Jamie?"

"I will," she says. "Should I hang up now?"

"Yes, you should hang up now and concentrate on driving back up here. Call me if you need me."

"I don't want to hang up. Can you stay on the line while I drive up there?"

"No, I need to call—"

"Oh, lord," she shrieks. "Somebody just pulled up to the pumps and this woman is going in, she's going in, she's gonna...I have to get out of here."

"Jamie?"

I hear the crunch of tires on gravel, then silence as the line goes dead.

Two days earlier

Jamie Lochner is something, I give her that. Tall, lithe, honey-blond hair in a thick French braid, perfect tan, three or four years on the right side of thirty, no obvious work on the face or body, dazzling in a white sundress that shows off gazelle legs to maximum advantage.

Just now she's perched in front of my desk at Jacinto Investigations, which happens to be in my redwood bungalow in the Cahuilla foothills of the San Jacinto Mountains. It overlooks the mosaic of country clubs, condos, and mansions known as greater Palm Springs. It's high enough and hard enough to reach that even two cops could afford it when I bought it with my late husband.

Jamie wants me to track down a guy named Tony Alvarez.

"And it'll be confidential, right?" she asks. A perfectly manicured nail flicks a blond lock away from a sea-blue eye.

"And Mr. Alvarez is?"

"A friend."

"Just a friend."

She nods.

"Okay."

"Y'all guys do that, right?" she says. "Find people?"

"You mean—"

"Private detectives. That's what you are, right?"

I'm primarily a legal investigator. Most of my clients are lawyers. It's one of them—Ike Skogel—who has sent Jamie my way.

But work is work, especially in a slow spell.

"Private detective is close enough," I say. "And, yes, we find people, mostly deadbeat dads, cheating spouses, people trying to skip out on debts or court appearances, that kind of thing. And we guarantee confidentiality. Especially from husbands."

She blushes a little. "How did you know?"

I point at her vacant ring finger. "The tan line."

She examines it for a moment. "I guess that should make me glad I came to you."

"Noticing things is what I do."

"So, yes, I'm married."

"And Mr. Lochner is very rich, I'm guessing from that Mercedes convertible in the driveway. Electric, right?"

"Of course. My aunt told me to marry well and divorce better," she says. "Or just wait if he's really old."

"And Mr. Lochner is old?"

She nods. "I thought I could do it."

"But an old man is not the same as a young one."

"Especially at night. Those liver-spotted claw hands on my..." She shudders and her eyes go a little dead. "At least it's only twice a month."

"Prenup?"

"Of course. Although lately, it's not even that often. He seems to have tapered off."

"So tell me about Tony," I say.

Her face relaxes into something that looks real rather than performed. Her eyes come back to life. "Can we just talk? I don't guess you have any Lone Star?"

"No beer. I do have wine."

"Maybe something white?"

"I'll see what I can do."

"And not with a metal cap if possible. Metal caps make me homesick for Lone Star. It's the only thing I miss about Texas."

I nod at the patio door across the living room. "We can talk out there."

She pulls out her phone and disappears toward the patio as I start for the kitchen. There I pour her a glass of chardonnay—from a bottle with a cork—and make an espresso for myself. I'm starting to like Jamie, but you have to be careful around a woman that beautiful. They tend to be snakes.

When I reach the patio, I discover that Jamie has made another conquest. My retired German Shepherd K-9 unit has his head on her knee and she's scratching him behind the ears. He's grinning in bliss, tongue lolling.

"I see you've met Duke." I hand her the wine.

"Duke," she says. "I like that. It's strong and masculine. And direct."

"He's all that."

"I just hope I don't disappoint him."

"Why would you?"

"You haven't heard my story yet."

"Duke doesn't judge."

"Do you?"

"Not while I'm on the clock." I say this with a just-us-girls vibe and wait to see if she picks up on it.

She does.

"Dana, I am so glad Mr. Skogel sent me to you," she says. "And that you're a woman, all things considered. He said you were a sheriff before."

"Deputy sheriff, actually. Out of the Brawley station."

Her face says she's never heard of Brawley.

"Other end of the Coachella Valley from Palm Springs? Slab City, Salvation Mountain, Salton Sea, that area?"

"The Salton Sea. I've heard of that. It's why Palm Springs smells like rotten eggs when the wind blows from down there." She sips the wine. "And Mr. Skogel said you're a widow?"

I nod. "My husband was a Palm Springs policeman. He was killed on duty."

"I'm so sorry."

"Me, too. Most of the time."

"Sorry if I was nosy." She rests her heels on the flagstones of the patio, then settles back in her chair. "So, Tony."

I raise my espresso cup. She looks puzzled for a moment, then raises her glass. We clink and drink. "To Tony," I say.

"Where do I start?"

"The beginning is usually good."

"Ever been to Luscomb, Texas?"

I shake my head.

"Lucky you. Officially has the second-highest murder rate in the state, which is going some in Texas. Probably the same for house trailers if anybody kept track. You ever hear that joke?"

"Eh?"

"How to tell if you're a redneck?"

"How?"

"Your house has more wheels than all five pickups in the yard combined."

"Good one."

"Anyway, I was raised in a house trailer by my Aunt Blue." The remains of her Texas twang make it sound like "ain't blue."

"She's the one who advised you on marriage and divorce?"

"That's her. Mary Bluebelle Harper. Mama left when I was seven and Daddy was always gone working the oil fields or drunk when he was home, so I got farmed out to Aunt Blue."

I raise my espresso again. "To Aunt Blue."

She bumps and says, "God rest her soul."

She's silent for a time. I think of asking what happened to Aunt Blue, but decide it doesn't matter.

"I was twelve when puberty hit and started to bloom," Jamie goes on, "Couple years later, Aunt Blue pulls me in front of a mirror and tells me to look at myself. I was already freaking out from the boys at Luscomb Middle School and even the math teacher Mr. Dunleavy trying to stare down my front all the time, and Aunt Blue knew that. 'Look,' she says. 'You see 'at face? 'Em eyes, 'em legs, 'at butt, 'em boobs? That's your ticket outta here. Don't waste 'em on some cowboy.'"

"I'm loving Aunt Blue a lot."

"Smart as a barn cat and twice as mean. I actually listened to her about saving myself so I could get out of Luscomb. With the teenage hormones and all, you wouldn't think it, but I did, I saved myself as long as I could. But then there was this one boy, Darren, he was so sweet, he was my first, and he wanted us to..."

She tears up and falters to a stop. "He had a pickup and a job in the oil fields and a couple horses and he wanted to have kids and teach them to ride and that's how he saw his life but I..."

"Yeah," I say. "It didn't—"

"That's right. It didn't seem like enough. So, I let Darren go. Broke both our hearts, second-hardest thing I ever did. I got myself an associate degree in business administration from the community college while I clerked part-time at the Walmart, then I told Aunt Blue I was heading for Las Vegas. Lot of rich men out there with money flying every which way was what I heard."

"But you ended up here."

"Uh-huh. Aunt Blue said I should come to Palm Springs instead. 'More rich old men and less hookers,' she told me. She has a half-sister out here, Anna Marie, that works housekeeping at the Agua Dulce, and she got me on as a cocktail waitress. Next thing you know I'm dealing blackjack. I showed a lot of cleavage, the players got distracted, my table was always hot and loud, and it made a lot of money for the tribe. Pretty soon I'm dealing VIP games in the private suites and on track for a pit boss job. Then one night Barney walks in."

"Barney being Mr. Lochner."

"King of the high rollers."

"And you were set for life."

"Looked like it," she says. "I worked him for a few months, Mr. Skogel negotiated a nice prenup, half a million on my wedding day, a quarter million every anniversary, twenty thousand a month to be president of Barney's racehorse charity, and another three million if we're still married when he dies. Plus I'm in the will for half his estate."

"He has a racehorse charity and you run it?"

"The American Thoroughbred Foundation. It's kind of a tax dodge, I think. He owns a couple of thoroughbreds through it."

"Wow."

She puts on a thin smile. 'That's life behind the velvet rope, but it's not all bad. I haven't flown commercial since I married Barney. All I have to do is sleep with him every two weeks, not fool around, and keep my BMI under twenty-two."

"That's in the prenup?"

"Pretty standard, according to Mr. Skogel."

"A fat trophy wife being an oxymoron?" I wonder if she'll know what that is.

She smiles again and nods. "Lucky for me, I have a hummingbird metabolism. And to be fair, Barney has kept his part of the deal, the money always drops into my account on schedule. But..."

"The liver-spotted claw hands?"

"Yes, I have to close my eyes and—"

"Dissociate?"

"I don't know what that is, but it sounds right. Anyway, Barney loves golf, it's a religion with these people, and he wanted me to learn because, you know, it goes with being a trophy wife and running the foundation and all. So I started taking lessons at our club. The Birdstone?"

"I've heard of it," I tell her.

That's putting it mildly. Everybody's heard of the Birdstone. It's the most exclusive country club in Palm Springs. The initiation fee is a quarter million, assuming you pass muster with the membership committee. The Birdstone even runs its own private jet service for members.

"So I go in for my first lesson, the instructor shows up. His name is Tony Alvarez and he so reminds me of Darren, the boy I knew in school..."

"Darren was Latino, was he?"

"I don't know," she says. "Maybe some, he kind of looked like it. But his last name was Ledbetter, so...I mean it's Texas and..."

"Anyway, Tony."

"Uh-huh. One look at Tony and suddenly I'm thinking about Darren and how you don't know how good the good times were till it sneaks up on you like that. You ever have that experience?"

"Who hasn't?"

"Call it nostalgia, hormones, whatever, but Tony felt like my second chance. Within a week we were hot and heavy, we went at it like horny teenagers for six months."

"Until?"

"Until Tony asked me to marry him. I told him I would divorce Barney when I got four million in the bank if he didn't die first, but I'm only up to three and that wouldn't be enough to support the kids I wanted to have, not and live like I'm used to now so..."

"So you let Tony go, too? And that was the first hardest thing you ever did?"

She nods. "He started crying and said he had to think about whether he could keep sharing me like that. Then he took off on the motorcycle I bought him and he never came back."

"And you thought you could live with it."

"For about five minutes. Then my baby bell started ringing and I realized Tony wasn't my second chance, he was my last chance. I would never be any good to any man or to myself if I was to stay with Barney. Suddenly I was done performing."

"Performing?"

She nods. "Be the smart girl in class so the teacher notices you. Be the pretty girl at the bar so the tips are good. Be the sexy dealer so the VIPs request your table. I'm really good at being what people want. So good I forgot how to be myself."

She looks out across the valley. "And then Tony looked at me like I was a real person, not the role I was playing, and I remembered what it felt like to just be Jamie. Not Trophy Wife Jamie or Hot Dealer Jamie or Good Girl from Luscomb Jamie. Just me, the one I'd been hiding since I was fourteen."

She sips chardonnay. I sip espresso, and let the silence ride. Sometimes that's the best way to get someone to talk.

"I tried and tried to get hold of Tony," she says at last. "But he blocked my number, then his went out of service. And his place is closed up."

She glances up from her wine and sees something in my face, I guess.

"You have any kids, Dana?"

"We couldn't," I say. "I couldn't, actually. But he could. And did with his mistress. Twins."

"Oh, Jesus."

"Yeah. And then the mistress got murdered and in the middle of the night a friend of his dumped the babies right about where you're sitting and told me what happened. It was the first I knew about any of it."

"How old are they now?" She turns and looks into the house through the patio doors. "And do they live with, um, you?"

"They're three now and no, the parents of my office assistant took them in."

"You're not in their lives at all? Because you know, aren't they all that's left of your, ah . . ."

"We're kind of getting off track here." I clear my throat and swallow some espresso. "So, Tony ghosted you and then what?"

"I'm so sorry, I didn't mean—"

I wave her off. "Let's talk about Tony."

"Of course. So I asked about him at the Birdstone. The pro shop wouldn't tell me anything."

"And now you want me to find him?"

She nods again.

"You know where he's from?"

"He wanted me to meet his mother in Indio."

She taps her phone and shows me a photo of a hunky Latino smiling cheek to cheek with a gray-haired woman with a grandma look. Tony's got olive skin, snapping black eyes, a huge smile, and scissor-cut hair.

"Sweet-looking boy," I say.

"It's been weeks, I tried and tried to talk some sense into myself, but I can't, I just can't. I have to see him again. Can you find him for me?"

"Sure, I'll find him."

"Will it take long? We're going out to Louisville for the Derby in a few days."

"Did you get the hat already?"

"Of course. And the dress. I took the Birdstone jet out there twice for the fittings. Plus, one of our thoroughbreds is in the race, *Barney's Best Girl*?"

"Sounds kinda like you," I don't say.

"I don't follow horse racing," I do say. "But, no, it probably won't take long, a day or two maybe. Men are lousy at hiding."

"Fingers crossed," she says.

"When I find him, what do I do?"

"Text me where he is so I can go tell him how much I love him and the answer is 'yes,' I'll marry him and we'll go to Mexico. With a border between us, maybe Barney will leave us alone. And I can get out of this costume and stop playing the hot girl."

"What about the Derby?"

"To hell with the Derby. And Barney."

Chapter Two

BEFORE JAMIE LEAVES, I extract a few details about Tony.

Very few. She doesn't know his middle name and assumes his first one is Antonio or Anthony. Nor does she know his mother's name—first or last—only that she lives in Indio.

She does know the address of his apartment in Palm Desert, on which she was paying the rent. But she's been there several times since the breakup and found nothing but the furniture that came with the place.

She also knows Tony's defunct cell number, but that's of little help. Not only did he cancel the phone, but there's no way to get location data from the phone company unless it involves a court case. A manhunt doesn't qualify.

There is the Harley Davidson Street Glide she bought Tony to replace his old Sportster. She has a photo on her phone of him on the new bike, with the license plate showing.

And that's it.

"I get eight hundred a day or two hundred an hour," I say. "Whichever is less."

"A couple of days, you said?" She brings up her phone. "You do Venmo?"

I nod, tap my phone to life, and show her my handle–@cahuillasleuth. She taps at her screen, my phone pings, and Venmo reports she's dropped in sixteen hundred dollars.

"*¿Bueno?*" she asks.

"Very *bueno,*" I say.

As she glides down Cahuilla Drive in the pale blue Mercedes, I open the patio gate to let Duke out for a bathroom break and a romp with the coyotes who prowl the brush behind the house. A breeze from the southeast has come up, strong enough to bend the mesquite and greasewood a little and swirl flurries of sand across the patio.

While Duke is busy out back, I point my computer at one of the private-eye databases I use. As I expect, the search for the license plate on Tony's Harley dead-ends at the address of his abandoned apartment in Palm Desert.

Half an hour later, I pull into the parking lot of Ike Skogel and Associates in a single-story beige complex on Tahquitz Canyon Way. I ease my middle-aged Grand Cherokee up beside his silver BMW—electric, of course–and try not to feel guilty for pumping out the CO_2 I do.

It's still early April but Palm Springs is already heating up—mid-afternoon and 97 degrees, according to the display in the Jeep. I spread foil sun deflectors over the dashboard, crack the windows half an inch, and dart like a roadrunner across the asphalt griddle of the parking lot.

Inside, Ike's office is cool, whisper-quiet and decorated with a subtle elegance calculated to intimidate the new client.

Glenn, Ike's pony-tailed receptionist, looks up as I come in, shoots a fast glance at his computer screen. "You don't have an appointment."

Ditto, the one-eyed office calico, is asleep in an Amazon box behind the sofa. He raises his head, gives me the once-over, and goes back to sleep. His box is next to the fancy cat bed Glenn bought him, but he refuses to use it. Ditto sleeps only in boxes.

"Do I ever have an appointment?"

"It would improve my quality of life." He waves me down the hall to Ike's office.

I can see through the glass door that Ike's on his phone. But the client's chair is empty, so I push in.

It turns out he's not on the phone per se. He's dictating a brief into it, something to do with a new ordinance clamping down on short-term rentals in Palm Springs. He talks machine-gun fast, sounds like he's reading from a law book, and works without notes. All while flipping a yellow pencil with his free hand.

"The Air-B-and-Begone case?" I ask when he finishes.

"What can I say, huge client with bottomless pockets," he says. "Just let me send this to Glenn to type up."

To look at Ike, you wouldn't think he belongs in an office this classy. Wiry hair, big ears, black-frame glasses on a long-nosed face with a couple too many teeth for the mouth. All atop a scrawny body with a voice that goes shrill when he's excited, which he usually is. And there's the pencil-flipping.

But he makes it work. Juries love him. So have a remarkable number of women, for reasons I've never understood. Maybe it's the energy. Or maybe they sense how much he loves women, despite how little he understands us.

He taps the phone a couple times, it swooshes, and he turns his attention to me.

"So," I say. "Jamie Lochner."

"Indeed. Has she got it going on, or what?"

"What she has is a rich husband and a lawyer who let her sign a prenup with a BMI clause."

"The other side insisted and she didn't mind."

"You should have minded," I say. "You're her lawyer."

"All she cared about was how many commas after the dollar sign, at least till she found true love on the golf course."

"Except now Tony's disappeared and she wants me to find him so they can run off together."

Ike shrugs. "I tried to talk her out of it, but she didn't hear a word I said. Women, am I right?"

I return the glare he deserves, then tell him the story Jamie told me.

"Liver-spotted claw hands," he says when I've finished. "Gotta say, I feel for her there."

"Save your tears," I remind him. "She's already banked three million."

"Good point. Coffee?"

"Sure, Americano with a whisper of cream."

He punches the intercom on his desk phone and asks Glenn to bring in two of them.

"So what can I do you for this morning?"

"Just wondering if there's anything I should know about Barney Lochner."

He leans back and twirls the ring. "Ah, yes, Barney. One thing I can tell you, he hires serious lawyers. Underscore 'serious.' Those prenup negotiations? Brutal. Especially on the BMI, the intimacy clause, and the infidelity clause."

"Huh. Maybe he found out about Tony and sent the serious lawyers around for a chat?"

"Could be," Ike says. "Maybe Tony's all about the commas, too."

"He took some money to take a hike?"

"Love's a beautiful thing."

Glenn glides in with the coffee, sets the tray down without rattling a cup, and vanishes.

"So who is he, anyway?" I ask Ike over the rim of my cup. "Lochner, the name rings a bell, but—"

"Yeah, the dean of the desert, they call him. Dripping rich, on all the right boards, in all the right clubs—"

"Like the Birdstone."

"Of course the Birdstone. And he chairs the fundraising committee for the museum or the Plaza Theater, I forget which, maybe both, donates to all the right causes."

"Ah, right." I say. "I think I've seen him on the news a few times. But I don't pay much attention to the have-a-lots. I'm more partial to the have-nots."

"Word to that," Ike says.

"How'd he make his money?"

"I don't really know other than the usual gossip. Retired here out of Phoenix a few years back, had been in construction, land development, water rights, I'm not sure what-all. When he got to Palm Springs, he started writing checks, cultivated the right people, now there's nobody in town that doesn't take his calls."

"You're a member at the Birdstone, right?"

"Strictly business," Ike says with a guilty look. "Some of these velvet ropers I have to deal with, they don't return your call unless they think you're one, too."

"Uh-huh."

Ike grins. "Gotta confess, I do like golf, and those courses at the Birdstone are sublime. Plus, it's deductible. But why the sudden interest?"

"Tony Alvarez didn't leave much of a trail, and I want to talk to his boss at the Birdstone golf operation."

"No problem," Ike says. "You want Bish Wilson. One of many useful people I take care of at Christmas. Let me give him a call."

Ike does, and Bish agrees to see me as soon as I can get there.

Chapter Three

AS I ROUND THE CURVE in the Birdstone's long arc of driveway, the gleaming white clubhouse comes into view. It's cut into the side of a ridge and looms up like an ancient cliff dwelling.

I steer the Jeep past rows of Beamers, Escalades, Porsches, and a matching pair of red Maseratis to park in front of the golf shop. It's at the west end of the clubhouse, beside the eighteenth green of one of the Birdstone's two courses. A foursome is teeing up in the slanting afternoon sun as I park.

I text Bish Wilson at the number Ike gave me. He meets me at the staff entrance. We exchange names and a brief handshake, then he walks me down a hall to his office. He waves me to a chair and slides behind his desk.

"How's my pal Ike?" he asks.

"What can I say? Ike is Ike. He was working the Air-B-and-Begone case when I saw him just now. Like chopping wood, he says, but it pays the bills."

"That's our Ike." Bish shows me a grin, wide and backed by big white veneers. "You a golfer, Dana?"

Bish is early forties, I'd guess. Lean, fit, golden tan, close-cropped curly brown hair, crinkly gray eyes. He's in a blue polo with the black and gold Birdstone logo on the breast. His wrist sports a gold Rolex, his ring finger a gold wedding band.

"Not really," I tell him. "My late husband Frank liked to golf, but I never got into it myself. I'm more of a hiker."

"Gotcha," he says. "I know golf's not for everybody. But for me, it's church."

"Really."

He nods with another grin. "Depending on who I'm playing, of course."

To one side of Bish's desk is a glass cabinet of golf trophies. To the other is a wall of photos from his PGA days—Bish with famous golfers, Bish with aging movie stars, Bish with a notorious rapper. There's even one of Bish with a fairly recent president, whom I point at.

"What about him?"

"Easy," he says. "I made sure he won, but not by enough he'd figure it out. You gotta know the fine art of sandbagging is all. He loved beating a pro and left a happy man."

"I'm sure he did."

"So. Ike says you're interested in Tony Alvarez?"

"I'm trying to track him down."

"He in some kind of trouble?"

"If you count woman trouble."

"Would the woman in question by any chance be Barney Lochner's wife?"

"I probably shouldn't say. We guarantee confidentiality."

"Neither should I," Bish says. "And we never had this conversation?"

"You talked to her?"

"Nope, but I definitely talked to her husband."

"Barney Lochner."

Bish nods. "He came storming in here, him and that daughter of his, told me Tony was sleeping with his wife and I needed to fire him. And he gave me a message for Tony: Tell the little shit that if he ever contacts her again I'll divorce her ass and leave her penniless."

"Ah."

"Barney's on our board, knows everybody worth knowing, serious guy. His wish is our command."

"Did he have any proof?"

"Oh, yeah—pictures of them going into an apartment together. The daughter showed me on her phone. Gotta say, I had to sympathize with Tony at that point. That Jamie Lochner's an eyeful, eh?"

I ignore the drooling. "So Barney put an investigator on them?"

"I got the impression the daughter did. Whatever, somebody definitely got pictures of them together."

"I take it you fired Tony, then?"

"What was I gonna do? I told him I'd throw in a month's termination pay and give him a good recommendation, but, yeah, he had to go."

"And he was okay with that?"

"Of course not, I mean look at her. But when I gave him the message from Barney, he threw in the towel."

"Did he say what he was gonna do?"

"His plan was to work for his uncle in one of those ghost towns down on the Salton Sea till he found something up north and we should mail his final paycheck in care of the uncle."

"He was gonna head north? What's up—"

"Golfing mostly shuts down in the summer here."

"Uh-huh," I say. "Frank used to bitch about it because he couldn't play except for a couple hours right after sunup or right before sundown."

"Right. So these guys follow the snowbirds north and work at the resorts up in Wyoming, Montana, Colorado—summer country."

"You got an address for this uncle on the Salton?"

Bish frowns and scratches his wrist. "Let me—yeah, Tony texted it to me and I passed it on to the business office. You want it?"

I nod and Bish punches a button on his desk phone. He tells someone named Serena to email him Tony's address.

"What can you tell me about Tony?"

"Decent golfer, but they're a dime a dozen around here. I hired him mostly for his looks."

"Really."

Bish nods. "Your average rich lady expects a good-looking instructor. We sell a lot of lessons that way."

"With benefits?"

"Strictly against the club rules, but some of 'em do figure with what we charge, they're entitled. Rich people are like that, you know? They don't have to care about money, they just want their asses kissed and don't waste their time."

"No wonder they like the Birdstone."

"Yep," Bish says. "We know what not to notice and everybody's happy as long as we put out little fires like this situation with Barney Lochner's wife."

"Anything else I should know about Tony?"

"Let's see, let's see." Bish massages the bridge of his nose. "He's from Indio, learned to play at the municipal course down there, had quite a reputation as a Skins hustler."

"Skins hustler?"

"You don't know about Skins?"

I shake my head and Bish launches into a long, complicated explanation of how Skins is a golf betting game where so many skins are assigned to each hole and then…and then I paste on an interested smile. Sometimes, the quickest way to a man's heart is to let him nerd out. Another situation where a woman is better off faking it.

Finally, Bish reaches the part about the last hole, which is that the player with the most skins gets all the money.

"And the rest get skinned, is that it?"

Bish nods and shows me the veneers again. "Supposedly the skins were originally animal furs in Scotland. But, yeah, Skins is as much psychology as it is putts and drives. And Tony was the best sandbagger I ever played with. He could read people like an MRI machine, especially on a golf course. He loved nothing better than skinning rich white guys, so I had to ban him from playing it here."

The computer on Bish's desk chimes. He checks his screen, then rotates it to show me the email he's pulled up. "There you go."

"Thanks," I say as I type Tony's address into my phone. "Riviera Dunes, huh?"

Back in the Jeep, I start the engine, lower the windows, punch the AC all the way up, and study Tony's address while the car cools down. Care of Manolo Alvarez, it reads. 14 El Monte Avenue, Riviera Dunes.

I pull up the map app on my phone and type in the address. 14 El Monte turns out to be Manny's Gas and Mini Mart. And there's a phone number.

I tap it and hope for female voice, or a male one too old to be Tony's. I'll ask for Tony, and if the response is some version of "Hang on, I'll get him," I'll tap off, text Jamie the good news, and refund most of her money.

Anything else, and I'll have to go down there.

Anything else it is. A robot tells me the number is no longer in service.

Riviera Dunes is about an hour southeast of Palm Springs on the west shore of the Salton Sea. That's doable today, but it is getting late. Already, the sun is skimming the crests of the San Bernardino Mountains across the valley from Palm Springs. Much of the drive down to Riviera Dunes and all of it on the way back will be in the dark, mostly on two-lane farm highways.

Plus, Manny's could be closed when I get there—the map app doesn't list the hours of operation—and then I'll have to find someplace to spend the night, which means I'll need to take Duke along, which means...which means not today.

When I get home, a silver Escalade is parked in the driveway. The windows are tinted, so I can't see in. But the taillights are on, which suggests it's idling, which suggests it's occupied.

I pull in to the left of it, lower my passenger window, and wait. The driver's window glides down and there at the wheel is a sharp featured woman with straight brown hair and huge brown-tinted glasses. A heart-shaped face ends at a pointed chin under a small mouth. The net effect is of a mosquito in human form. She holds an unlit cigarillo in one hand and has a phone pressed to her ear with the other. She raises the cigarillo hand in a give-me-a-sec gesture, says "Okay, gotta go," and lowers the phone.

"I'm Nielle Lochner," she says. "Daddy would like to speak with you."

"Daddy?"

The Escalade's rear window whirs down and I see an old man in a white cardigan, dark glasses, and a green golf cap from the Birdstone. He puts a gloved hand on the sill and leans out.

"Dana Forsythe?"

"Uh-huh."

"Barney Lochner. Can you get in?"

Nielle steps out and around the SUV to open the opposite passenger door for me. I climb in across from Barney and sink into the creamy yellow leather of the back seat.

It's cool, dark, and rich inside the SUV. In the muted light, with gloves covering the alleged claw hands, Barney looks pretty good—silver hair, stubble beard, that air of unshakable self-assurance you get with rich men of a certain age.

He sips from a tumbler of amber liquid on the rocks and gives me the once-over from behind the dark lenses. The seat between us has been replaced by a small built-in bar. It holds a decanter of the amber liquid, along with ice and another glass. Barney doesn't offer me any.

"How can I help you, Mr. Lochner?"

"They say you're the best private investigator in Palm Springs."

"Who does?"

He smiles softly and waves a gloved hand. "People I know. It doesn't matter."

"Okay."

"Point is, I need to know something."

"What would that be?"

"Who's embezzling money out of my racehorse charity."

"How do you know anybody is?"

Another wave of the hand. This time it trembles a little, just a quick jitter, barely noticeable. He notices me noticing, and the hand steadies. "I know," he says. "Otherwise I wouldn't be here."

"But you don't know who?" I ask.

"Apparently they know how to cover their tracks."

"They usually do, for a while."

"I'll pay two thousand a day if you can come up with the proof."

"I'm afraid I have to pass. I'm all booked up right now."

"Five thousand a day?"

"Sorry, still no."

He turns the dark lenses on my house, then on me again. "Got a conflict, do you?"

"Thanks anyway."

"Uh-huh."

I open the door and step out. Nielle is leaning against my Jeep and putting in eye drops. The cigarillo is now lit and dangling from a corner of her mouth.

"Will you be joining us?" she asks as she pockets the eye drops.

"Nope," I say. "Too busy."

"Your loss." She stubs the cigarillo out on my tire and flicks it into the sand beside the driveway.

The Escalade backs out and pulls away as I heel-kick a hole in the sand and bury the cigarillo butt. Duke, I see, has been watching from the front window of the house, ears at full alert.

When I get inside, I let him out for his morning business, which today starts with an investigation of the driveway. First he sniffs around the spot where the black SUV was parked, then the spot behind my Jeep where Cigarillo Woman stood when she asked me about joining the team. Finally, he lifts his leg over the spot where I buried the cigarillo, then trots off into the brush.

I go in and build myself a Moscow mule in a copper mug, drop into a chair on the patio and start dialing.

No, Bish has not heard from Barney, and doesn't know how Barney heard about me.

Nor has Ike Skogel spoken with him. But he's not surprised to hear that Barney knows about Jacinto Investigations.

"I always pass along one of your cards if somebody asks me about getting a legal investigator," he says. "So, yeah, your name is around town."

"Still seems like quite a coincidence," I tell him. "A husband and wife both try to hire me the same day?"

"It's the desert, Dana," he says. "These things happen."

My next call is to Jamie.

"What!" she almost shrieks when I break the news. "He knows!"

"It could be a coincidence."

"Bullshit! He knows."

"And there's more, actually."

"More?"

"It turns out Barney got Tony got fired because of you—"

"That asshole, I knew it! But why would that matter? Tony knew I would love him whatever happened."

I tell her about Nielle's investigator and the photos he got. "And Barney told Tony's boss to tell Tony that he would divorce you and leave you penniless if Tony ever contacted you again."

"But he did contact me and he asked me to marry him and my answer made him think all I cared about was the money."

She waits like she expects me to offer comfort. I don't.

"Oh, lord, what should I do?"

"Up to you. I can stop looking for Tony if you want to stay home and be a good little trophy wife and inherit a serious fortune someday. It is what you signed up for. And let's be realistic. If you take off with Tony, Barney will do what he threatened and send you home to that trailer in Luscomb, with or without Tony, with nothing but the clothes on your back and a change of underwear, if that."

"But won't he do it anyway if he already knows about Tony?"

"Good point. Have you hidden your assets?"

"No," she says. "I didn't think that far ahead and I wouldn't really know how, anyway. I guess I was in—"

"In, yeah, love. Love does that to people. Well, talk to Ike and see what he can do. You want me to call it off with Tony?"

"Can you find him?"

"I think I may already have." I tell her about tomorrow's trip to Riviera Dunes. "But feel free to go yourself. I'm happy to bow out now."

"No, no, you go. Barney's going to LA to see his doctor and I'm gonna talk to Mr. Skogel and see if we can hide my money before Barney realizes I'm gone. The next day, if you find Tony I'll—"

"You'll make your getaway."

Chapter Four

I JUMP ON THE PELOTON and take a news cruise on my tablet while I sweat for half an hour. There's an update on the city's latest effort to keep blowing sand from shutting down Gene Autry Trail, the main connector between the Palm Springs airport and the Interstate: a two million dollar brick wind wall. The local desert rats are quick to point out that the roadsides along Gene Autry are littered with the remains of previous wind walls. A guy named Hugo Gaviota quotes Einstein to a reporter from the Palm Springs Herald: "Insanity is doing the same thing over and over again and expecting different results."

After that, I take Duke out for a stroll before dinner. We're a few yards from the house when a coyote yips and Duke vanishes into the brush. I'm on the sofa watching a game show on cable when he noses the patio door open and comes back in. He's happy all over—tongue lolling, tail wagging, a big smile on his face.

"Prefer coyote company over mine do ya, buddy?"

I scratch his rump and he wiggles it in a way that I don't tell him is undignified for a big scary police dog.

I'm not ready for dinner yet, so I hit the Peloton for a hard half hour, then the shower. As happens sometimes, the icy spray, particularly on the back of my neck, revs me up rather than slowing me down. Luckily, I know a guy.

I grab my phone off the vanity, step onto the patio naked and dripping, and take a quick shot of the San Jacintos back of the house as they turn orange and purple in the sunset. Then I bring up Cinder, attach the picture, type "Another beautiful night in the desert. REALLY beautiful!" and send the message on its way. Thanks to Cinder it'll vanish in a day, opened or not, from my phone and his.

The guy in question is Luther Velasco, better known as the Chaplain because that's his role in the Moguls biker gang. The problem is, he's not easy to get hold of.

For starters, he never lets anyone call him. If I try, he buries his current burner phone in the desert and switches to a new one. You don't call the Chaplain, he calls you.

And he operates only at night. He's a police informant, so he can't be spotted near anyone from law enforcement, not even an ex-cop and cop's widow like me. If that happened, his fellow Moguls would plant him in the desert sand garden with his old burners.

How then to get in touch? Send a "beautiful desert" message on Cinder, and wait. That's the rule.

The Chaplain was a bequest of sorts from my late husband. Frank was the Chaplain's handler at Palm Springs Public Safety and he asked the Chaplain to look after me if the worst happened to him.

The worst did, about a year and a half ago. A few nights later, the Chaplain showed up on my patio at 3 a.m., told me the deal, and said to put up the "beautiful day in the desert" signal if I ever needed anything.

I was slow to buy into it. But then I retired from police work and became a private investigator. It turned out that requires more of the Chaplain's kind of help than I expected.

Now he's my confidential informant, witness retriever, and secret go-to for things best done in the dark. Which lately has included spending an occasional night in my bed. I'm not sure I trust it. But he's six and a half feet of biker menace, muscle, and comfort and I like how his beard scratches my neck. I don't overthink it.

Once I asked him about the Chaplain thing. "Bikers have spiritual needs?"

"Everybody does," he said. "Most of them are as broken as me."

How long will I have to wait for his call? There's no knowing. It could be ten minutes or ten hours. Once it was four days and I thought he was dead, but it turned out to be only because he needed to leave his phone off so he couldn't be tracked.

If he doesn't call there are other ways to solve the problem. But when my body reminds me that I'm a female animal, nothing but a male animal will do. I go back inside, pull on a silk robe and throw together another Moscow mule. I'm halfway through it and trying to decide what to do if he doesn't call, when he does.

"What's happening, *cariño?*"

"What's happening? Way less than I'd like. Where are you?"

"Half an hour away, maybe less."

"The less the better."

His familiar knowing chuckle raises my temperature even more, then the line goes dead. He never says goodbye.

Back to the patio and I stand in the dusk debating whether to drop the robe so there'll be nothing but moonlight between me and him when he arrives. No, I decide, keep it on. He likes to handle the unveiling himself.

I drop onto a chair and sip on the mule for what seems forever. Finally I hear the mutter of his Harley coming up Cahuilla Drive. It rounds the corner of the house—headlight off—and stops beside the patio.

Then his arms around me, the smell of leather and maleness, his beard tickling my neck, his whisper of "I missed you, *cariño*."

When I return from wherever it is I go at such times, he's on his back smoking a Partagas, I'm spooned against his side, my leg draped over his.

"That cigar reminds me of Frank."

He takes a puff, inspects the Partagas. "He got me started on them."

"Uh-huh."

"Is that a good thing or a bad thing, to remember Frank?"

"Just a thing, I guess. Everything reminds me of him."

"Uh-huh." He draws on the Partagas in silence.

"I talk to him sometimes."

"Frank? *¿Realmente?*"

"Yes, really. The memory of him that lives in my head. I call him Imaginary Frank."

"What do you talk about?"

"Sometimes us."

He rolls on his side and we lock eyes. "What does he say about us?"

"He thinks I should let this happen. He says we can save each other."

This produces a long, reflective silence. Then, "I hope so. How are his twins?"

"Thriving," I tell the Chaplain. "The adoption's moving along, they love Lita and her parents and they love pre-school, a place called Brighter Day. Rose likes numbers, Sonny likes art. He drew that picture of Duke on the fridge. I spend half my nights with them down in Chapel City or Lita brings them up here."

"I'd like to see them again."

"I'll let you know some night when Lita's bringing them up."

"That would be good," he says. "As long as they don't stay too long, *verdad?*"

He bites my neck again.

"Absolutely not," I say as I roll on top of him.

Sometime later, when I'm collapsed and sweating, the twins are still on my mind. "Yolanda—that's Lita's mom—is a better mother to Sonny and Rose than I ever could have been. Or Jennifer, according to Imaginary Frank."

"She tried," he says. "In her way. What do you do when they come up here?"

"Take little hikes out back. Go down the mountain for ice cream. Watch *Peppa Pig* on TV. Sleep in a heap in my bed."

"All of you?"

"Yep. Like African wild dogs. One big pile of love and cuddles."

"How do you get them to sleep?"

"I read them *Goodnight Moon*. Never fails."

"*Goodnight Moon?*"

I sit up in bed. "The greatest children's story ever written. Your mom never read it to you?"

"She never read me anything."

"Never? What—"

"What's so great about *Goodnight Moon?*" he interrupts.

Translation: "Don't ask me about my mom." I should have known better.

"If you could explain it, it wouldn't be great," I say. "I'll read it to you."

I flip on the bedside lamp, pull the book from the nightstand, open it to the picture of the baby rabbit in its bed, and begin with maybe the most famous lines in kiddy literature:

In the great green room

There was a telephone

And a red balloon

I finish with "Good night moon and good night noises everywhere." And then I start bawling.

"*¡Jesús!*" he says. "What was that?"

"All women cry when they read *Goodnight Moon.*

"*¿Todas?*"

"Yes, all of us. Trust me."

"But why?"

"It's about how children need to know they will wake up in the same world they went to sleep in," I say. "And women, we know it's up to us to make that happen."

"And Frank's kids, their world was turned upside down twice. First him, then their mother."

"Shut up or I'll start again. Let's change the subject."

"Okay."

I get up and pad into the bathroom to sort myself out.

"Working on anything much?" he asks when I return.

"Maybe, yeah." It's a relief to tell him about the rich old man with liver-spotted claw-hands, the love-starved trophy wife, and her search for redemption in the arms of the Harley-riding Skins hustler.

"I think I've tracked him down," I conclude. "He gets his mail at Manny's Gas and Mini Mart in Riviera Dunes. So I'm going down there tomorrow."

"Manny Alvarez? I remember him. He had a tooth missing in front. He'd clamp his jaws shut and put his cigarette through the gap to make us kids laugh. He said he was a dragon."

Of course he would know Manny Alvarez. The Chaplain's from Solipatria, which is a few miles from Riviera Dunes. Everybody knows everybody at the south end of the Salton Sea.

"I heard he had cancer," the Chaplain goes on. "Maybe he died."

"I hope not. But whatever, his Mini Mart is where Lover Boy gets his mail."

"What's his name?"

"Lover Boy? Tony. Tony Alvarez."

"Him I don't know. But that's Moguls country. If he rides a Harley, he'll be on their radar. I could ask around."

"If you like. But mainly, I just want to find him and be done with these people."

***

Morning comes and the Chaplain's gone. No goodbye, which is fine with me.

There's enough wind to turn the sky steel gray with blowing dust, but otherwise it's not a bad day for a drive. After breakfast—yogurt, melon, and granola for me, Blue Buffalo for Duke—I let him out for his morning business and throw a few things into a backpack for the trip to Riviera Dunes.

When I head out to the Jeep, Duke's already back from the brush and sniffing around the rear bumper.

"What's the matter, buddy?" I ask him. "Your coyote pals marking your territory now?"

He looks at me and whines.

"Don't come crying to me, it's not my problem."

He gives me another reproachful look as I shoo him back inside and lock up.

My route is down the west shore of the slow-motion ecological disaster known as the Salton Sea. The Salton is beautiful enough today, a shimmering expanse of lazy swells and sun-kissed blue that conjures up visions of resorts, marinas, girls on water skis, and the waterfront mansions of plutocrats from Palm Springs and celebs from Los Angeles.

And the Salton had all that once upon a time, thanks to water brought in via canal from the Colorado River. Then the water got diverted to farms and to cities like LA and Palm Springs, and the Salton began shrinking.

Now, it's a stinking toxic sump. The mansions are falling in on themselves, the marinas are hundreds of yards from the shrinking shoreline, the resort cities are crumbling monuments to broken desert dreams.

Riviera Dunes is one of those dreams. It sits on a patch of sand and mesquite between the highway and the Salton. Manny's Gas Station and Mini Mart is on El Monte Avenue a few blocks in, past scattered houses and mobile homes. Nearly all are surrounded by chain-link fencing and padlocked gates, and many are decorated with FOR SALE signs. So are most of the vacant lots between them.

I pull the Jeep up to the lone fuel pump at Manny's, pop the gas cap, and put the nozzle into the filler neck. The Mini Mart is a single story of weathered wood and faded red paint. A rusted sign on the front says they're open from seven to midnight, and the one next to it says they take EBT cards. Beside the window is a pay phone with no receiver, probably the one the robot told me was no longer in service.

I'm hoping Tony will come out to see if the lady needs assistance, but no such luck. However, parked beside the building is a near-new Harley Street Glide with a FOR SALE sign duct-taped to the headlight.

I walk inside and there's Tony behind the counter, looking even hotter in real life than in the picture on Jamie's phone.

I pull two packages of salted almonds off a rack that also offers the sketchy over-the-counter painkiller called ZaZa. It's also known as highway heroin because you can find it at gas stations and it may or may not be a mild opioid. I drop the almonds and a pair of twenties beside the register. "Put whatever's left after the almonds on the pump, okay?"

"*De seguro.*" He smiles and rings it up.

"*Gracias.* That your Street Glide out there?"

"Yeah." He pushes a receipt across the counter. "I'm gonna miss it."

"Things tight, are they?"

"Ah, you know, I came down here to help my uncle while he's in Mexico for his cancer, but this place..." He shrugs at the unpromising prospects around him and waves away a fly dive-buzzing his face. "Sometimes it's everything all at once, *sí?*"

"Every time, right?"

He chuckles. "*Sí,* every time."

"So it's just you here?"

"Just me. Good thing my uncle has burritos in the cooler and a bunk in the back room."

"Had the bike long?"

"Few months," he says. "Not even 4,000 miles yet. You interested?"

"Asking for a friend," I tell him. "I could mention your name."

"Sure, why not? Tony Alvarez." He puts out a hand.

"Lana Flores," I say as we shake. I'm not Latina, but I have enough desert tan and sufficiently ambiguous features to pass as mixed-race when I need to. Plus, people in the desert know not to ask a lot of questions.

"You got a number I should give him?"

"Sure." He scrawls it on the back of the receipt.

"Thanks, I'll let him know."

While I'm fueling the Jeep, a bearded guy in a big white testosterone pickup pulls up beside Tony's Harley and gets out for a look. Tony emerges from the mini mart and walks over as I put the nozzle back into the pump.

I watch from the driver's seat as the two of them discuss the bike. Testosterone Guy climbs on and kicks it to life as I dial Jamie's number.

"I'm looking at Tony right now," I tell her.

"Already?" There's a catch in her voice.

I lower the window a couple inches and hold the phone up to the opening as Testosterone Guy revs the Street Glide up to a pretty decent thunder. "Hear that? It's the Harley you bought him. He's trying to sell it."

"Oh, no. He loves that bike."

"Maybe what you're gonna tell him will change his mind. I can hand him the phone. Or I got his new number, if you want to call him."

"No, no," she says. "It has to be in person. I want to surprise him."

"It's a place called Manny's in Riviera Dunes," I say. "I'll text you the address and Tony's phone. Just put it in your map and you'll be here in less than an hour."

She pauses. "Not today. I'm meeting with Ike about shielding my assets."

"Oh, right."

"I'll pack a bag tonight after Barney goes to bed and take off first thing in the morning before he's up. I'll leave him a note saying I have a spa appointment. He won't miss me till it's too late."

A male voice sounds in the background, too low to understand. Jamie semi-shouts, "It's nothing, love, the spa about my appointment tomorrow."

"Manny's opens at seven," I say.

Chapter Five

IT'S 8:13 A.M. when my phone pings and Jamie's ID pops up on the screen and she shrieks, "He's dead!"

Then I hear the crunch of tires on gravel and the call drops, I stare into space and imagine a fly crawling into Tony Alvarez's beautiful nose.

I shake it off with a shudder, get out of bed, let Duke out for his morning excursion into the brush, start an espresso in the Keurig, and head for the shower.

Half an hour later, I pull in at Skogel and Associates. Ike opens the door and ushers me down the hall to his office. The business day hasn't started yet, so it's just the two of us.

"Jesus Christ," he says as he slides in behind his desk. "What the hell is this?"

"You said that on the phone."

"So is she coming up here or is she headed for Texas?"

"She isn't picking up. Let me try her again."

This time she does pick up.

"Are you coming back to Palm Springs?" I ask.

"I am now. But I still might turn around."

"Don't do that."

"I'm scared to death. If he, if Barney killed Tony, if he did that means I'm next and I, I—"

"Jamie, you do not know who killed Tony. Do not go to Texas. Come to Ike's office."

"The map in the car says I'll be there in 19 minutes." The call drops.

Ike flips a pencil into the air and catches it.

"Is she in trouble for not calling 911 on this?" I ask.

He squeezes the bridge of his nose with one hand and keeps the pencil going with the other. "Not under California law. You're not legally required to report a crime, unless..."

"Unless what?"

"Unless you were involved but then of course there's the Fifth Amendment. So, no."

"You think she did this?"

"I don't know what I think."

"I mean, the theory would have to be, she drives down to Riviera Dunes, shoots Tony, and the first thing she does is call me? How much sense does that make?"

"It's love," he says. "Anything's possible. You need to tell me everything that happened after I set you up with Bish."

I tell him how I tracked Tony to Manny's in Riviera Dunes, what Tony said, and what Jamie said when I called her with the good news.

"And the rest you know," I conclude. "So, again, the theory would have to be that Jamie's master plan was to get her lawyer to refer her to an ex-cop now practicing the ancient and honorable profession of snooping into other people's sex lives, then hire said ex-cop to lead her to her one true love so she could kill him. After which she calls me to report his demise?"

"Well, when you put it that way." He falls into a reflective silence.

As do I.

"What if..." he says, and stops.

He sips his coffee. I sip mine.

"Or maybe..." I say, and stop.

More silence, more coffee.

"Unless Tony turned her down," Ike says finally. "No fury and all that? And that story is how she plans to get away with it?"

"Huh."

He pushes a button on his desk phone and says, "Glenn, could you come in for a moment?"

Glenn arrives with a carafe and two cups, and pours.

"Thanks," Ike says, "but that's not it. We have reason to believe there may have been a homicide in Riviera Dunes this morning, victim by the name of Tony Alvarez. Will you see what you can find on the computer or by phone?"

"I know a hot deputy in the sheriff's office down in Brawley," Glenn says. "I think they cover Riviera Dunes."

"They do," I say. "Everything around the Salton Sea."

Glenn nods and steps out. We hear the TV in the front office come on.

"He's checking the news, too," Ike says. "Good kid."

"So where were we?"

"This is a complicated situation," he says. "Jamie's a potential suspect. She's a witness, too, obviously. And because she is, you are."

"I was afraid of that. So what do we do?"

There's another stir out front, then the sound of a woman shrieking too fast to follow. Then Jamie is peering through Ike's glass door and looking like hell. Mascara streaking her cheeks, lipstick half chewed off. When a woman like Jamie gets out of a car without checking her makeup, you know it's serious.

Ike waves her in. She fumbles at the knob, can't make it turn, and slides down the opposite wall of the hallway. She buries her face in her hands and collapses into sobs. Ike starts to rise.

"Let me," I say.

I grab the box of tissues on Ike's desk, go into the hallway and drop down to the floor beside Jamie.

"Hey, sweetie," I say as Ike watches through the glass. "How about a little touchup?"

She snuffles, rubs her nose on the back of her wrist, turns to me, and closes her eyes like a child.

I wipe her nose, dab the mascara off her cheeks, dig into the Gucci minibag on the floor beside her, and find a tube of Tom Ford lipstick. It is, of course, the perfect shade of coral for her blond hair, blue eyes, and brown mascara.

I repair her lipstick and put the tube back in her bag.

"There we are." I pat her wrist. "Do you want to go in and talk to Mr. Skogel now, or do you need a moment in the ladies room?"

She wraps her arms around my neck and squeezes so hard it hurts. We sit like that as she sobs a few more times. "I love you, Dana," she says. "You're like Aunt Blue. She always knew what to do."

I pat one of the arms around my neck and say, "There, there, sweetie. We'll figure something out."

The sobs taper off. She lets go of my neck and settles back against the wall. "I guess I could talk to Mr. Skogel now."

"Okay."

She doesn't move.

"Do you want to talk to him out here?"

No answer.

Glenn materializes with a mug of steaming tea. "This is lavender, Mrs. Lochner," he says. "But we have chamomile or—"

Jamie takes the mug and sips. The dry sobs resume.

I mouth a silent "thank you" and wave Glenn back down the hall.

The sobs abate as Jamie sips the tea. She still hasn't moved from the floor.

"Maybe we should stand up now?"

After a period of thought, she does, and without spilling any tea. I help her into the office while Ike hovers at a safe distance.

When we're settled in our chairs, he clears his throat.

"Jamie," he says, "I don't know what's going on here, but the police will be wanting to talk to you. Do you want me to represent you?"

She nods.

"Actually," he says, "a verbal response would be better."

Jamie's face says this is too much to process just now.

"He needs you to say 'yes' out loud," I say.

"Yes," she says. "I want you to represent me."

"Very well," he says. "We'll take care of the paperwork and some other details in just a bit here."

She nods, then says, "Okay. Yes."

"And I would like Dana to be my investigator in this matter," Ike says. "Would that be acceptable to you, Jamie?"

"Yes," she says. "I love Dana. Of course I want her on my ca-ca-case."

The word 'case' undoes her. More sobs. She grabs a tissue from Ike's box and dabs her eyes.

Ike shoots me a look. I raise my hands in a let-her-be gesture. When she's calm, Ike speaks again.

"If you do want her as our investigator, the first thing you need to do is fire her."

"What?"

"You have to fire Dana. It's cleaner that way. She can't work for both of us."

Jamie gives a short, bitter laugh. "I guess she's done what I hired her for. Dana, you're fired."

"I'll refund most of your retainer."

Another bitter laugh. "That's the least of my problems right now."

Ike clears his throat again.

"Jamie, if you choose to talk to the police, they will ask what happened at Manny's, including if you killed Tony. As you may know, you're free to refuse to answer that question, or any other question you feel could incriminate you. Even if it comes from me."

Jamie straightens in her chair, and the sad, flat eyes blaze up. "What? No! Of course I'll answer it. I did not kill Tony. I loved Tony. How can you even say something like that to me?"

"Sorry," he says. "It's part of the job."

Jamie looks at me, eyes wide in question.

I nod. "He's right."

"One more detail," Ike says. "We'll get you a suite at the Parsons while we sort this out."

"No way, Jamie says. "I'm staying at the mansion like nothing happened. I want to see their faces when I walk in."

"That's insane," Ike says. "How can you act normal when you think—"

"I've been acting normal ever since I married Barney," Jamie says. "I don't even have to try now. And maybe I'll find out how they did it."

"Bad idea, Jamie," I say. "Maybe the worst one I ever heard of. My advice is you should—"

"Did I ask for your advice?" she says.

Chapter Six

THREE DAYS LATER the Coachella County Sheriff's Office is coming to interview Jamie.

"Jamie," Ike says as we await their arrival. "One more time: you do not want to talk to the police."

"And one more time, yes, I do. I know Barney and Skeeter killed Tony and I want to tell them that."

"You do not know who killed Tony, and you especially do not know it was your husband and his daughter," Ike says. "Because you've been at the mansion three days and even you admit you've seen or heard nothing that gives them away."

"I know what I know," she says. "And I will talk to the police."

At 9:30, right on time, we hear voices in the outer office, then Glenn shows in a cop.

He's Sergeant Ray Jefferson, a homicide investigator and former colleague of mine in the Brawley sheriff's office. He's in uniform and almost a hunk. Strong solid face you want to trust, stubble beard, thinning brown hair, just the right amount of dad bod.

I introduce Jefferson and he passes over a business card.

"And this is Jamie Lochner," Ike says from behind his desk.

Jamie smiles from Ike's side. Her blonde mane is pulled into a tidy bun today and she's in a severe black suit over a white top.

White high heels complete the ensemble. It says, "Yeah, I'm hot, but this is strictly business."

Jefferson nods as he takes a chair in front of Ike's desk. "Mrs. Lochner."

"We'll be recording this interview," Ike says.

I start the video camera we've set up a few feet away, then take a seat on the leather sofa in the corner, notepad on my knee.

"Likewise, " Jefferson says. He sets a digital recorder on the edge of the desk and pushes a button. He reels off the names of all present for the benefit of the recorders, followed by Jamie's Miranda warning.

"And one note before we start, " Ike says, "I've advised Mrs. Lochner against granting this interview, but she insists."

"Of course I insist," Jamie says. "I have nothing to hide."

"Good to know," Jefferson says. "Much appreciated."

He opens his notebook to a blank page, and looks at Jamie. "Mrs. Lochner, how about you just tell me in your own words what happened the day Tony Alvarez's body was discovered at Manny's Mini-Mart in Riviera Dunes."

Jamie gives him the short version, as hashed out by the three of us over breakfast at Sheldon's. We've rehearsed it again in Ike's office before the interview, complete with a stern warning from Ike: "Stick to the facts, no guesses."

"And you left for Riviera Dunes exactly when?" Jefferson asks when she's done.

"Around 7 am."

"And who was in the residence at the time?"

"Just my husband, as far as I know. The housekeeper doesn't show up till 9 or 10, usually, and Skeeter, that's Barney's daughter, sleeps in till 8 or 9. She lives in the pool house."

Jefferson nods. "So there's an ALPR a couple—"

Ike interrupts. "That's a traffic camera, Jamie. They take a picture of your license plate as you go by."

"Correct," Jefferson says. "The Palm Springs police have one a few blocks from the Lochner property at a traffic light on South Palm Canyon. It shows your car going through there at, let's see, 7:08 am."

"Sure, that sounds right."

"And the county has one at the Indio exit from Interstate 10, where you pick up California 86 to Riviera Dunes. You went by that one at, ah, at 7:39."

This fog of detail is a message to Jamie: Don't even think about lying.

She shrugs. "I was on my way to see Tony."

"So another traffic camera caught you at 8:11 as you went through the traffic light at the turnoff from Route 86 into Riviera Dunes and continued on, I assume, to Manny's, ah, Manny's Gas Station and Mini Mart. So you would have gotten there, say, around, 8:15, does that sound right?"

"What does the exact time matter?"

"This is a murder investigation, Mrs. Lochner. Everything matters. But tell us, exactly and in detail, what happened when you got to Manny's."

"I'll try," Jamie says. "But I—"

She buries her face in her hands and draws deep shuddering breaths. I pass her a tissue and she presses it to her eyes.

"Take all the time you need," Jefferson says in a tone that sounds sympathetic but is pure Interrogation 101. "There's no rush."

"Tony and I were lovers," she says after a long pause. "He had asked me several weeks before this to leave Barney and marry him, but I turned him down. I was going to tell him I changed my mind and I would be his wife if he would still have me."

She falters to a stop again. I bring her a bottle of Fiji water from the refrigerator in the break room. She uncaps it, sips twice, and sets it on the desk.

"So I pulled up to the pumps and waited for Tony to come out," she says. "I wanted to see the look on his face when he saw my car. He didn't come out, but I thought he must be there. His motorcycle was parked next to the building and there was an "OPEN" sign on the door and the lights were on inside."

She stops and sips from the bottle. "So I went in. I didn't see him anywhere, so I called his name. There was this door behind the counter I thought might be a stockroom or something, so I went around to check in there and he...he...he was..."

Another breakdown, another pause, more Fiji. Jamie's eyes flatten and her lips thin out to a line of grim resolve.

"He was back there behind the counter dead and there was blood everywhere and I thought "I'm having a nightmare" but...but...but I, I bent down, I knelt down, and I felt the side of his neck to see if he was...but he wasn't, he wasn't breathing and there was all this blood, I looked at my hand and, and...and there was a fly in his nose."

She stops and holds up her right hand and stares at it for several seconds. "And there was blood on it, blood on my fingers, and I remember looking at the blood and thinking, 'I should lower my hand or it will run down into my bracelet and I'll have to have it cleaned.' It was a bracelet, this silver bracelet Tony gave me, he said it was his mother's, and when I thought about how his blood would be on his mother's bracelet, that's when I knew he was dead. Or I guess I knew it when I touched him, but that's when it hit me that he was and I, and I...and there was a fly in his nose."

Jamie falls silent. Jefferson gives her some time, then, "Can you tell us where he was shot?"

"I don't know, there was so much blood. Around his head, and two or three places on his shirt, I don't know, I couldn't look anymore after I saw the blood on my hand."

She raises the hand and studies it again. More silence from Jefferson.

"I'm so sorry for your loss," he says finally. "Then what did you do?"

Jamie keeps studying the hand.

Jefferson clears his throat. "Mrs. Lochner?"

Jamie wrenches her eyes away from the hand. "I went back to my car and called Dana. Mrs. Forsythe."

"Why would you call Mrs. Forsythe?"

"Because I hired her to find Tony and she did and she told me he worked at Manny's and I didn't know what else to do when I found, when I found his...when I found him."

"You didn't think of calling 911?"

"No, I was just, I wasn't myself, and this woman pulled up on the other side of the pumps and I just took off, I think I hit her car when I turned and I—"

"Yes, you did hit her rear fender," Jefferson says. "Nadine Warbelow, lives in a trailer in Riviera Dunes. She stopped at Manny's on her way to work at the prison in Solipatria to get a breakfast burrito and some ZaZa for her sciatica. After the—"

"ZaZa?" Ike interrupts. "Highway heroin?"

"She does use Tianeptine." Jefferson says. "But it is legal in California and Ms. Warbelow claims to have run out of it the previous day. That's why she was buying it at Manny's. We do not believe she was under its influence at the time of the collision upon her arrival."

"Noted," Ike says with his crocodile smile.

Jefferson looks a little nervous as he continues. "Ms. Warbelow made a video on her phone as you took off, then she went in and found Mr. Alvarez's body and called 911." He checks his notes. "8:22 is when she called. The video she took of your Mercedes caught the last three letters of your license number and that's how we identified you as a person of interest in this matter."

"Yeah, but I didn't kill Tony. I know—"

"Our coroner estimates, from the rectal temperature, that Mr. Alvarez was shot pretty close to the time of your arrival, Mrs. Lochner. A half hour at most."

"I don't care, I—"

"So you can see why we're here," Jefferson says. "You didn't see anybody around Manny's, leaving Manny's, anything like that as you drove up?"

She shakes her head. "Nobody. But I wasn't looking anywhere but at the Mini Mart, because I wanted to see Tony."

"Let's backtrack for a moment. How exactly did you come to hire Mrs. Forsythe here?"

"Mr. Skogel recommended her."

Jefferson's gaze swings to Ike, who doesn't react. "Mr. Skogel?"

"Uh-huh," Jamie says. "He negotiated my prenup with Barney, so I asked him about hiring a private investigator to find Tony and he recommended Dana."

"And Mr. Skogel, if I have this straight, Mrs. Forsythe is now your investigator in your representation of Mrs. Lochner in this matter?" He squeezes the bridge of his nose. "And I'm guessing you're not going—"

"You are correct. Mrs. Forsythe will not be discussing any aspect of this case with you. Everything she knows or has done in connection with the matter is privileged."

"Except there was no case until Mrs. Lochner retained you the morning of Mr. Alvarez's murder. Up to that point, Mrs. Forsythe was working for Mrs. Lochner on an unrelated matter, correct?"

"Yeah, right," Ike says. "Unrelated."

"We could get a court order," Jefferson says.

"You could try."

"All right, let's talk about the murder weapon," Jefferson tells Jamie. "You're right that Mr. Alvarez was struck by three shots. To be specific, two to the chest and one to the head. Two in the chest to take him down, we think, then a head shot to make sure."

Jamie shudders, but doesn't speak.

"So we ran these bullets through ballistics, and we've established they came from a .22 caliber weapon."

Jamie is still silent.

"Is there anything you want to say at this point, Mrs. Lochner."

She shakes her head.

"Well, it turns out that a Ruger LCR 22 revolver was purchased last year at a Palm Springs gun shop and registered in your name. Do you have anything to say now?"

"Barney bought me that gun. It was after the old woman from Vermont was robbed in that home invasion last fall? They almost beat her to death?"

This produces nods and "yeahs" from Ike and Jefferson. The Palm Springs economy depends on snowbirds. Robbing and beating them is bad for business, very bad. The perpetrators were arrested within hours, and confessed the next day.

"Yeah, Barney got kind of paranoid after that. So he got me the little Ruger and took me out in the desert by Joshua Tree and taught me to shoot it. Where they have all the abandoned cars?"

More nods and "yeahs," and she continues.

"We shot up a bunch of 'em for target practice. I had my gun, he had his, it was a lot bigger and a lot louder than mine, I remember that. And he called it the Terminator. From some old movie, I think." She pauses with a look of surprise. "That was a fun trip, actually. One of the few good days I've had with Barney. He said I was the sunlight of his twilight. After that, he put in a firing range in the basement for practice, so we never went out there again. Anyway, I keep my gun in the console of my car."

"A ballistics test could clear this whole thing up," Jefferson says. "You mind if we—"

"Hold on," Ike says. "Do you have a search warrant?"

"No, but with what she just said, we can get one in about—"

"Take the gun," Jamie interrupts. "I don't care. It didn't shoot Tony."

"Jamie, here's the problem," Ike says. "Ballistics tests can rarely establish with certainty whether two bullets were fired by the same gun, just that it could likely have been the same gun because of similar markings. And there's a million of those little Rugers around, which makes the problem even worse. You let them test your gun, the chances are approximately one hundred percent they'll come back and say it's consistent with being the murder weapon and you'll be arrested."

Ike looks at Jefferson. "Right, sergeant?"

"That's an oversimplification," Jefferson says. "But regardless, we'll get a search warrant and take the gun anyway. Why make it harder than it needs to be?"

"Let's go," Jamie says.

"Jamie!" Ike says.

She heads for the parking lot and we follow her to the blue Mercedes.

She unlocks it with the fob, then bows to Jefferson with a sweep of her arm. "Be my guest."

Jefferson leans in and paws through the console. "You said it was in here, Mrs. Lochner?"

"It's not?"

Jefferson goes through the glove compartment, then backs out and checks under the seats. "Mind opening the trunk for me, Mrs. Lochner?"

"Why would it be in the trunk?" she says. But she clicks the fob. The lid rises.

Jefferson does a quick but thorough job of tossing the trunk.

He straightens and looks at Jamie. "No gun."

"It never leaves this car except when I practice in our basement firing range."

"Sorry, ma'am."

"Oh, Jesus," Jamie says. "Oh, Jesus."

"Ma'am?" Jefferson says.

"Jamie?" Ike says.

She starts to sob. "Barney took it. He took it out of my car and he killed Tony with it because he knew how much I loved him."

"You just told us your husband was asleep when you left for Riviera Dunes," Jefferson says. "How could he possibly—"

"I don't know how, but he did. Or maybe Skeeter did it. She's a Daddy's girl and she hates me. One of them did it, or they did it together, I know they did."

She folds herself into my arms and weeps mascara onto my shoulder. I pat hers. All I can think of to say is, "Easy, sweetheart. Easy."

Jefferson chews his lip. "Mrs. Lochner, we, need to—"

"What you need to do is investigate Barney Lochner and his daughter," Ike says. "This interview is over and—"

"Ike, you have to come in here! Ike!"

It's Glenn yelling at us from the office door.

"We're a little busy out here," Ike yells back.

"Right now, Ike. You have to see this."

We follow Ike into the front office. A Palm Springs channel is up on the wall-mounted TV. It shows a drone shot of emergency vehicles with flashing lights pulled up at the gate of a walled estate with a sprawling midcentury modern mansion. The gate has the initials "BL" monogrammed onto the ironwork.

Jamie shoulders her way to the front and gapes at the screen. "That's my house!"

The estate is surrounded by tall, elegant date palms and a wall draped in gorgeous purple bougainvillea, except for the gaps where "ARMED RESPONSE" security signs are posted. Before one of them stands a TV reporter, microphone in hand.

"All right," says a studio announcer in voiceover, "I think...yeah, we have Ron Abrams on the scene now, and apparently he has been able to get some information on what we are told is the shooting death of Palm Springs philanthropist Barney Lochner. Ron, are you—"

The shot cuts to ground level in front of the gate.

"Yeah, Jeanette," the reporter says. "Yeah, the police aren't saying anything official yet, but our producer down here was able to get a comment from someone close to the situation, and what we are being told is that Mr. Lochner died in his study this morning from multiple gunshot wounds."

Jamie shrieks, "What the hell?"

On the screen, I see a Palm Springs homicide investigator I know, Gary Avila, coming up the drive toward the gate. He's talking with a uniformed officer leading a police dog. The gate slides open and they step through.

Ron sticks his mike in Avila's face. "Lieutenant, lieutenant, can we get a statement? Is the victim really Barney Lochner? What happened here?

Avila shoulders past him without comment. The camera follows him as he climbs into an unmarked. The officer with him puts the dog into a K-9 SUV and both vehicles pull away. The camera swings back to Ron in front of the gate.

"Well, as you can see, Jeanette, the police aren't saying much about what went on here at the Lochner compound this morning. So I guess it's back to you."

That's when I notice the mosquito-faced woman in big brown sunglasses walking up the drive toward the gate.

So does Jamie.

"Skeeter," she breathes. "That's Skeeter!"

"Ron," Jeanette says from the studio, "I think you've got somebody behind you there, I don't know what—"

Nielle Lochner reaches the gate. It slides open as Ron turns to see what's going on.

"You," she says. "Come over here."

Ron does, and sticks out his microphone. "Who are—"

"I'm Barney Lochner's daughter," Nielle says. "And I know who shot him."

"What? Who—"

"It was that gold-digging little slut he married," she says. "I tried to warn him but the damned old fool thought he was in love and now she's killed him. And she used the gun he bought her! I saw that police dog find it!"

She turns and marches back down the drive. The gate slides shut as Ron shouts, "Ma'am! Ma'am, wait, what's your name? Did you witness the murder?"

Chapter Seven

"ANYTHING YOU WANT to tell us Jamie?" Ike says once Jefferson's gone and Glenn has supplied us with coffee and tea

He hovers at the door in an advantageous position for eavesdropping until Ike shoos him away and shuts us in.

Ditto, for reasons known only to himself, likes me today. He's left his box and jumped onto my lap. Now he purrs and drools as he digs his claws into my thigh. I want to swat him off, but I'm afraid he'll do something worse. That one eye of his freaks me out.

Jamie sips chamomile and dabs at her nose. "As I told you at breakfast, Barney called me into his study this morning because he had something to tell me."

"And he told you he wanted to divorce you," Ike says.

"Right," she says. "But I didn't really go into all the details then because, you know, we were planning what I would tell Sergeant Jefferson. I thought we could talk about what Barney said later."

"And now it's later," Ike says. "To put it mildly. Let's hear those details.

"He said he knew about Tony and me and called me a cheating little whore," she says. "He said he was divorcing me, and he hoped I'd be very happy in my little trailer in Texas with a yard full of brats because I wasn't getting another nickel of his money. And not only that, he and his lawyer were going to claw back what I already got."

Ike scrawls a few lines of notes, and nods. "And you said?"

"I said he was lying because I knew he killed Tony and he said, 'What, Tony's dead? Such a shame, I'm so sorry.'"

"Wow," I say.

"Yeah," Jamie says. "I told him not only was he going to jail because he killed Tony, but also he wasn't getting any of my money because Mr. Skogel was already drawing up my own divorce papers, plus he's hiring us an asset provision attorney—"

"Actually," Ike says. "It's an asset protection attorney, a woman from San Bernardino named Isabel Uribe. The crypt-keeper, they call her."

"Right," Jamie says. "Asset protection attorney. I told Barney we were hiring one and he wasn't getting a cent of my money. Lord knows, those claw hands, I earned every nickel."

She shudders.

"Okay," Ike says. "And that was when you shot him?"

"Why would you say that. Mr. Skogel? You know I didn't."

"At the moment, I don't know what I know or what I think," Ike says. "But I know what Lieutenant Gary Avila from Palm Springs Public Safety is going to think."

"I don't care what he—"

"Jamie, you need to hear Ike out," I say. "Trust me on this."

"He's going think when Barney said he'd divorce you, you killed him so you'd still be married when he died and get that last three million under the prenup," Ike says.

"I guarantee that's what he'll think," I say. "And if that really was your gun the police dog found, you'll be arrested."

"And I'll do my best at trial but you'll probably be found guilty if it is your gun," Ike says.

Ike tilts his head and gives Jamie the look that I've seen make more than one witness forget what he was supposed to say and blurt out the truth despite himself.

Not Jamie.

"Well, that's bullshit," she says. "Pardon my French, but I did not shoot Barney with my gun or any other gun. But I'm glad the rotten bastard's dead. If they ever do arrest whoever did shoot him, I'll pay for their defense."

Chapter Eight

IT'S ANOTHER THREE DAYS before the police come to interview Jamie about Barney's murder. Three brutal days. Local reporters are like flies on the story, and Barney's enough of a big shot nationally that his killing gets play on the cable channels and broadcast networks. They call him not only a philanthropist, but also the owner of one of the favorites for the Kentucky Derby, *Barney's Best Girl*.

The Lochner compound is locked down as a crime scene, Jamie's been tested for gunshot residue, and her phone, laptop, and Mercedes have been taken into evidence. She's moved out of the mansion and is hiding from reporters at the Parsons Palm Springs—gated, exclusive, over a thousand a night, and across Palm Canyon Drive from a Mercedes dealer, a BMW dealer, and two trailer parks.

The reporters do find Ike and me and hound us till they realize "No comment" means "No comment."

But that doesn't stop the endless looping of the video of Nielle's show-up at the gate with her claim that Jamie shot her father. In less than a day reporters have dug up the love triangle and established Jamie as the link between Tony's murder in Riviera Dunes and Barney's death in Palm Springs. The hot photo of Tony from Jamie's phone has gotten loose and is all over the news, as well as social media. A couple of pod bros are calling Jamie "Barney's Fatal Filly."

The only exception to my personal no-comment policy is my gal-pal Liz Hernandez, the crime reporter for the *Palm Springs Herald*. We've been trading info since my days as a deputy with the sheriff's office. Her call I do take when her ID lights up my phone the day after the murder.

"I hear you're working for the defense in the Lochner murder," she says after we get the how-ya-beens out of the way.

"True," I tell her, "but I can't say much yet."

"Off the record, did the trophy wife really shoot him with the gun he bought her?"

"Nice try," I say. "If you had that nailed down you'd have printed it already instead of trying to schmooze a confirmation out of me."

"You know I won't say where I got it."

"Because you're not gonna get it, at least not from me. Sorry, but I just don't have anything I can share yet, even off the record."

"But when the time comes you will, right?"

"When did I ever not? And the margaritas are on me next time we hit the Outrigger."

"Deal," she says.

By the time the police show up at Ike's office a little before 10 on the third day after Barney's murder, we know from the news coverage that they don't need much from Jamie. What they plan, we assume, is to arrest her unless we have something that will change their minds. We assume we don't.

We hear voices in the outer office, then Glenn shows in three cops.

One them is Ray Jefferson from Brawley.

With him is Gary Avila, the cop in the now-famous "gold-digging slut" TV clip from Barney's gate. He's a homicide lieutenant from Palm Springs Public Safety, tough, rumpled, dark thinning hair, acne-pocked face. Jeans and jacket, loose tie on a white shirt, scuffed brown loafers, medium gut, no nonsense. He worked with my late husband, he knows the whole story of Frank's mistress and her twins, and I hate the pity in his eyes as he takes a chair in front of Ike's desk.

The third cop is a uniformed female officer whom Avila introduces as Dominguez. There's only one possible reason for her to be here.

After the introductions, Jefferson and Avila take chairs in front of Ike's desk. Dominguez, all business with a tight helmet of steel-colored hair, stations herself near me on the leather sofa.

Jefferson sets his little recorder on the desk, pushes the start button, and advises Jamie of her rights.

"And a note before we begin, Lt. Avila," Ike says, "I've advised Mrs. Lochner against granting this interview, same as with the earlier interview with Sgt. Jefferson. But once again she insists."

"I absolutely do," Jamie says. "Fire away."

"Mrs. Lochner," Avila says, "would you mind telling us what you did on the day your husband was shot, starting with when you got up, whatever interactions you had with him or anyone else, that kind of thing?"

Jamie repeats the story she told us the morning of Barney's death, including how she'd stayed at the mansion in hopes of getting evidence he killed Tony.

"So why would I kill my husband?" she concludes. "I wanted him alive so you guys throw his ass in jail where he belonged. He's who you should be investigating."

"Come on," Avila says. "There's just no evidence your husband had anything to do with Tony's death. Not one shred."

"You should hire Dana," Jamie says. "She would prove it."

"Not an option, sorry. But to get back on track here, you and your husband threatened to divorce each other and he said he would take all your money for violating your prenup because of your adultery, is that right?"

Another nod.

"And at the conclusion of this argument, you left and came here for your interview with Sergeant Jefferson?"

"Well, I came early to meet with Dana and Mr. Skogel to plan what I would tell Sgt. Jefferson in the interview."

"That was around 7:40, 7:50," Ike says.

"I think I left the mansion about 7:30," Jamie says.

"Who else was there at the time?"

"Just Barney in his study, as far as I know. Skeeter I assume was still asleep in the pool house. Like I told you before, she doesn't get up till 8 or 9, then she goes out to get bagels for Barney, so she wasn't in the mansion yet. Also like I said before, the housekeeper comes in around 8, so she wasn't yet, either. I think the landscapers were coming that day, but they don't arrive till midmorning, sometimes noon or later, and, anyway, they're not allowed inside the mansion."

"Of course not," Avila says.

Jamie catches the edge in his voice. "We let them use the restroom off the laundry room," she says. "And the housekeeper feeds them lunch on the pool deck."

"Uh-huh," Avila says. "And the housekeeper is Alina Kuznetsov, correct? She was the one who found Mr. Lochner's body and made the 911 call." He checks his notes again. "At, ah, here it is, at 8:04 am."

"Okay," Jamie says.

"And your husband that day," Avila goes on. "He was planning a trip to Los Angeles, is that right?"

"Correct. I don't remember exactly what time, but later in the day. Around 11, I think. Skeeter was going to drive him to the airport."

"Ah," Avila says. " We were already on scene when she arrived at, ah, 8:43 with the bagels from Sheldon's Deli."

He consults his notes again. "Anyway, the coroner's office conducted a preliminary examination of your husband's body. Based on the rectal temperature as measured at, um, let's see, 9:43 am, they put the time of death somewhere in the 6:45 to 8 o'clock range."

Jamie is silent.

"The same time frame you were leaving," Avila says.

He doesn't ask the obvious question here. He just waits.

Jamie waits, too, gaze steady on Avila.

"So how would that have happened? That your husband would be shot more or less as you were leaving for your meeting with Mr. Skogel?"

"How would I know how? Like I said, I didn't shoot him. Maybe somebody was hiding in the mansion or on the grounds? It's a pretty big compound, three or four acres, I think, a lot of landscaping with shrubs and hedges and palmettos. It wouldn't be hard."

"But it's surrounded by a security fence and there's video at the front gate. How would they get in? There's no sign of a break-in."

"Again, how would I know? The landscapers and the housekeeper have cards for the gate and I don't know who else got them over the years before I married Barney. And that ridge behind the mansion is undeveloped land, some kind of park or preserve with hiking and biking trails. It would probably be easy to come in through there and put up a ladder and climb over the wall. And that place has I think six doors. Maybe one of them was unlocked."

"But there's an alarm system, right?" Avila says.

"Right," Jamie says. "Motion detectors inside for when we're away, and what is it, insertion detectors, on—"

"Intrusion detectors?" Avila asks."

"That's it," Jamie says. "Intrusion detectors on the doors and windows whether we're there or not, plus panic buttons in several of the rooms."

"But no video?"

"Not inside, Barney wouldn't allow it. He thought it would end up on the Internet. The alarm system is with Coachella Security and they were always saying we should have video, too, but Barney wouldn't do it except outside on the front gate. He figured that plus the alarm system in the mansion and the armed response signs were enough."

"So, to summarize, you left home at 7:30 and drove to your meeting with Mr. Skogel and your husband was alive when you left. Is that it?"

"Yes, Barney was alive in his study. How many times to I have to say it?"

"But he was dead by 3:04. Any idea how that would have happened?

"No, but I didn't shoot him."

"Okay," Avila says. "Let's talk about the murder weapon. You saw the shitshow at the front gate on TV, according to Sgt. Jefferson, so you know our K-9 unit found a gun. And it was your Ruger."

"Where was it?"

"You tell me."

"Oh, please."

"It was buried under a palmetto behind the mansion," Avila says. "About 25 yards from the rear door."

"Buried how?" Ike asks.

"Apparently with a garden trowel from a wheelbarrow next to the palmetto."

"Fingerprints on the trowel?"

"None usable." Avila reaches into his jacket and drops a four-by-six photograph on the desk. "This is what the dog found."

I come up from the sofa for a look. The photograph shows a small revolver laid out on a white background.

Jamie nods. "That looks like my gun."

"Fingerprints on it?" Ike asks

"Only hers and Barney's," Avila says.

"From when he taught her to shoot it?" Ike asks.

"Presumably. Anyway, ballistics tells us in was in fact the same gun that killed Tony—"

"I went through this with Sgt. Jefferson," Ike says. "All ballistics can say for sure is, it could have been any one of the thousands of Ruger 22s in America."

"That's an overstatement. But it was found on the property," Avila says. "And it was Mrs. Lochner's gun with her fingerprints on it."

Avila turns to Jamie. "All the evidence we have is consistent with your gun killing your husband and your lover. In addition to which, they died the same way: two shots to the chest followed by an insurance shot to the head."

Jamie is silent.

"Same gun, same pattern," Avila says. "If not you, Mrs. Lochner, then who?"

"Obviously Skeeter," she says. "Or otherwise whoever stole my gun out of my car. But. It. Was. Not. Me!"

Avila thumbs through his notebook. "You continued staying at the Lochner mansion after your lover was murdered, correct?"

"Of course."

"And why was that?" Avila asks. "I mean, considering that—"

"I wasn't going to let them know I knew about Tony. And I was hoping they'd let slip how they killed him."

"Or was it because you were planning to kill Mr. Lochner because you believed he killed your lover?"

"I told you already, I didn't kill him. Although he did deserve it, the murdering bastard."

"But you would agree, it has to be the same person for both murders, right?

"It could be two diff—"

"Same gun and same MO? Too much coincidence."

Jamie is silent.

"Mrs. Lochner, this was a love triangle and you're the only member still standing." Avila rises and pulls a set of handcuffs from his belt as Dominguez moves up from the sofa. "Jameson Jean Lochner, you're under arrest for the murder of Barney Lochner."

"And for the murder of Tony Alvarez," Jefferson says. "Come out here, please."

She shoots me a terrified look from her chair beside Ike. "Do I have to? Can they—"

"I'm afraid they can," Ike says. "Just cooperate and I'll try to get you out on bail."

Jamie rises and comes out from behind the desk.

"Put your hands behind you, Mrs. Lochner," Avila says.

She does, Jefferson cuffs her, and Dominguez starts the pat-down.

***

"Well," Ike says.

We're at the front office window, watching Dominguez put Jamie into the back seat of a Crown Vic with Palm Springs Public Safety Department insignia.

"Well," I say as they pull away.

We settle onto Ike's sofa and I rack my brain for something profound to say. The best I can do is, "What now, boss?"

"Good question," Ike says. "I still think I probably have a guilty client. We told Jamie she was nuts to stay at the mansion, but she did it anyway. Avila could be right about the reason for that."

"Except she'd have to be nuts to think she could get away with killing Barney. She left a trail of evidence a blind man could follow."

"Maybe she was so pissed she just winged it," Ike says. "Figured she could charm her way out of it like beautiful women always do."

"I still don't think it makes sense."

"Murder rarely does," Ike says. "If killers were capable of rational thought, there'd be way fewer murders and we'd both have boring jobs. On the other hand, at least I wouldn't have to deal with homicidal trophy wives."

"But I'd be busting shoplifters at Walmart."

"There is that," Ike says.

"So, again, what now?"

"I think we have to let it go to trial."

"Should I start interviewing witnesses?" I say. "The help at Barney's mansion. Skeeter? The lady in Riviera Dunes whose car Jamie banged up?"

He waves it off. "Leave it till we see what they file in court. There's a million other things I need to be working on right now."

"If you're sure."

"And we could lose, you know. A guilty verdict would void the prenup and anything Jamie gets in the will, and the daughter will no doubt go after whatever Jamie's got in the bank. She could end up not just in prison, but also broke. We might never get paid."

"There is that retainer she gave you."

"Even a million dollars won't be enough for a trial like this. Like I said, it's a rich-people murder case. We gotta hire our own experts, probably specialty lawyers for various issues that will come up, appeals that drag on forever if she's convicted, I hate to think about it. Anyway, let's not spend any of Jamie's money on it until we need to. Bail alone will probably be at least a million. And that's if I can get her out at all."

"Seriously?"

He nods. "We're dealing with two counts of first-degree murder here."

"How about I at least background Barney and the daughter?"

"Okay, yeah," Ike says. "And I'll see what I can do on bail. Other than that, we let it play out."

Chapter Nine

WITH JAMIE IN JAIL and Ike working to bail her out, I've got nothing immediate on my calendar. I've been more or less nonstop on the Jamie Lochner case for better than six days. It's time for some downtime, which means a news cruise.

Today, the city police chief is blasting immigration cops for the latest raid. This time the target is Taco Tio's Mexican Grill, a beloved Palm Springs institution in a shopping plaza a few blocks west of downtown. "You're supposed to bust terrorists and bang on cartels," the chief says in an Instagram post. "Instead, you're doing jump outs and arresting dishwashers and gardeners."

Most of the commenters agree with him, including the snowbirds. You don't have to spend much time in Palm Springs to realize the economy would collapse without immigrant labor. And, let's face it, the number of Anglos willing to trim hedges in the hundred-degree sun approximates zero.

Enough drama for the day. I open my phone and tap Lita's contact.

Yes, she's home, and, yes, she'd love an outing with the twins.

A few minutes later, we're ordering cones at Cool It Ice Cream and Gelato in downtown Palm Springs. Pistachio for Rose, chocolate for Sonny, strawberry for Lita and me.

As usual, Rose is wearing a princess dress and her gap-toothed smile. Sonny's in cargo shorts and a t-shirt with a fire engine on the front.

As we wander out onto the sidewalk, Rose tugs my hand in her solemn way. *"¿Tia?"*

I drop into a chair at a table in front of Cool It and lift her onto my knee. "Yes, love."

"Can we go in the moon store?"

Which is what she calls Forever Books because it's where we bought *Goodnight Moon*. It's a couple doors down from Cool It.

Forever Books used to be Books Forever. Then the city brought in Forever Marilyn, a 26-foot statue of the late movie star with her skirt billowing up over a subway grate in the famous scene from *The Seven Year Itch*. The owners changed the name of the shop to Forever Books and put up a shelf of books about Marilyn, because capitalism.

"Sure, baby," I tell Rose "But let's eat our ice cream first so we don't get it on the books, okay?"

Rose nods and goes to work on her pistachio. Lita goes into Cool It, comes back with a wad of napkins, and takes the other chair at the table. Sonny climbs onto her lap and we lick away in the midday heat, which is a little above 90 at the moment. At least we're on the shady side of the building, so it's not unbearable yet.

We finish our cones, Lita cleans the kids up, and we go into the bookstore.

Sonny grabs a board book about firefighters. *Fireman Frank*, it's called. He takes a chair at a kid-sized table and opens it.

"They all want to be warriors of one kind or another," I say. "Ninety percent of the boys who come to my door at Halloween are still Darth Vaders."

"We should expand their horizons," Lita says. "Encourage them to be doctors and teachers."

"Good luck with that," I say. "It's primal programming."

"Then we should reprogram them."

"You can't fight DNA."

"At least Sonny wants to fight fires instead of people," Lita says.

Sonny brings us *Fireman Frank* and points to the spotted dog sitting behind Frank. "Dalmatian!" he says with much pride.

"That's right, Dalmatian!" Lita and I tell him simultaneously. "Very good, Sonny!"

"Can I get it?" he asks.

"You bet."

"Maybe it's just the Dalmatian he likes," Lita says as he goes back to the firefighting books.

"Whatever. As long as he doesn't want to be a cop like his father."

Lita, wise woman that she is, says nothing.

"And look at that," I give Lita a nudge and point at Rose standing transfixed before a shelf of Barbie books.

"So fake." Lita sneaks a glance at her hips. "She's a stick with *tetas*! Any woman with that waist would starve to death because the food couldn't get through. They did a study! And those high heels! And she doesn't even have a vagina! What kind of message does that send little girls?"

"Every little girl wants to be a princess."

"At least they grow out of it," she sighs. "I loved Barbie myself when I was little. Especially Latina Barbie."

"Maybe they'll bring out a gay Barbie." .

"Ha!"

Rose comes over with two Barbie books. In one, Barbie's a doctor. In the other, a champion horsewoman. To be fair, Barbie nowadays is way more about careers and adventures than babies and boyfriends.

Rose tugs my hand with the same serious expression as before.

"I want to marry Barbie," she says. "Can I get these?"

"Of course, baby," Lita says. She puts the books on the table.

"Marry Barbie, huh?" I say as Rose returns to the Barbie shelf. "I wonder where she gets that."

"Shut up. Sylvia and I never discuss it with her, I swear."

Sylvia being Sylvia Webster, Lita's fiancée and an extremely rich and divorced Palm Springs radiation oncologist.

"Uh-huh," I say. "Never."

Lita just grins. While the kids are busy, I show her the video of Jamie's interview with Avila. Then I tap my phone off and give her a moment to process.

"My god!" she says. "It's not possible."

"Tell me about it," I say. "None of it makes sense. Why would she kill either one of them, let alone both?"

Lita rests her chin on her hand and closes her eyes in thought. Then, "Huh."

"Huh what?"

"Maybe what Avila was saying. She already thought Barney killed Tony when she went to see him. Maybe she just lost it from what he said."

"And just happened to have her gun in her purse?" I ask.

"Allegedly."

"Agree, allegedly, but the dog did find it at the scene."

"Which does zero to explain why she would kill Tony." Lita pauses. "Huh."

"Huh what?"

"Maybe Tony had enough of skinny white girls and found himself a nice thick Latina," Lita says. "So when Jamie shows up and says she'll marry him after all, he turns her down."

"Or maybe said Latina is behind the counter giving him a day-brightener and Jamie—"

"*Sí*," Lita says. "*Sí*. And when Jamie sees that, she loses it and shoots him."

"But not the new girlfriend?"

"Maybe she was too fast."

"Maybe she got away while Tony was zipping up."

"And by the time Jamie finished shooting him," Lita says, "she was long gone."

"You should probably call Sergeant Jefferson," I suggest. "Ask him about the state of the corpse's zipper when Mrs. Warbelow discovered the crime."

Which undoes both of us. When we finish laughing, Lita says, "Or maybe there is no new girlfriend."

"And we're back to square one."

"What does Ike say?"

"You know him, strictly business," I tell her. "He says not to log any more time on this case except for backgrounding the Lochners. After that, there'll be weeks to months of pre-trial back-and-forth and we'll follow up on whatever information dribbles out."

"You said dribbles out."

This sets us off again. We compose ourselves with ice cream.

"So bottom line," I say. "Was it Jamie or not?"

"You know I don't trust rich white girls."

"You are about to marry one."

"Sylvia is different."

"Said only every love-struck maiden in the history of heart-break."

"Whatever," Lita says.

"And what about grandchildren? You know how your mom feels about that."

"I told her we will have two by artificial insemination," Lita says.

"And she said?"

"She said, 'From a test tube? No. Estrellita! I want real babies!'"

"That's our Yolanda," I say. "But I could ask Ike to help if you want to go old-school."

"Huh. Really? You think he would—"

"Pretty sure," I say. "But not with a test tube. The regular way."

Lita shakes her head with an expression of prim disapproval. "Shut up, we have to talk about the case. There is so much evidence against this Jamie. And people in love do strange things. But something makes me want to believe her."

"Same here, actually. So, listen, I'll background Barney and you take the daughter, this Nielle. She drove Barney to my house that day and Jamie says she spent a lot of time at the mansion. She has to know what was going on in that place."

"*Bueno.*"

"Oh–and I'll check in with the Chaplain. When I told him about Jamie hiring me to find Tony, he said he'd poke around."

"You said poke around," Lita says. "I guess we know why you want to see him."

We're still laughing when my phone lights up.

"Speak of the devil," I say as I bring up the call and head for the sidewalk.

"You don't have to leave," she says. "I'll plug my ears."

"Who's plugging their ears?" the Chaplain says as I step away.

"Lita, in case we're gonna talk dirty. Are we?"

"Not right now. That guy Tony Alvarez?"

"You heard, huh? He got shot and Jamie Lochner—"

"He was looking for somebody to take care of a gringo *rico* up in Palm Springs."

"Take care of a rich white man? As in kill?"

"*Sí*. It's all over the grapevine down here since he got shot."

"Jesus. What was—"

"Meet me at the windmills around one."

"But wait, how—?"

Too late, he's gone.

***

A little after midnight, I hit the road for the 45-minute drive through a dark and sleeping Palm Springs to the wind farm just south of Interstate 10. It's five till one when I park at the No Trespassing sign. The Chaplain pulls up on his Harley in the moonlight, lights off as usual. I slide on behind him, wrap my arms around his chest, and breathe in his smell as he noses the bike around the sign and starts across the sand. Riding bitch, I know from my cop days, is what bikers call it when a woman does this. But nobody better ever say it to my face.

A quarter mile in, he cuts the engine, and it's just us, stars, moonlight, and a ghost forest of windmills. Plus the sound they make—like the low throb of a distant locomotive mixed with the hum of a window fan in the next room. We swing off the bike and lean against the seats, gazing over the lights of Palm Springs to the peaks of the San Jacintos.

He's a big, bearded silhouette in the night, his voice rumbling deep in his chest. And in mine.

"When that guy Tony got killed," he says, "I got interested. Because you were involved, *sí?* I'm wondering, what did you get yourself into this time?"

"Same here, to put it mildly."

"*Sí.* So I have this cousin who's doing time in Solipatria."

"For what?"

"Doesn't matter. But he's one of the people I talked to about Tony getting shot. Did the girl really do it, or what? Couple days later, I get word I should come back again. And my cousin tells me Tony was looking for a hitman to take care of a rich gringo in Palm Springs."

As I digest this, the Chaplain pulls a cigar and a kitchen match from his vest, strikes the match with his thumbnail, and lights up.

"A hitman."

He nods. "To take care of a rich white man in Palm Springs." He puffs on the cigar and I catch the smell of a Partagas. "And now, such a man is dead."

"As is the guy who was looking for the hitman," I say. "He was killed first."

The Chaplain draws on his cigar. "And if you're a hitman, why kill the target if the customer is dead? Why not take the money and the win?"

"And the police say they were both killed with Jamie's Ruger. How would that happen?"

The Chaplain blows ash off the tip of his cigar. "None of it makes sense."

"We have to find out if this hitman is real. Your cousin in Solipatria told you what exactly?"

"Tony's half-brother is in there for dealing," the Chaplain says. "Jesús Medina. Jesse, they call him. Tony passed word through Jesse he was looking for a hitman. It got around the prison."

"And he found somebody?"

"Who knows?"

"Maybe Jesse would?"

"Probably. But he's not talking. Too risky with Tony and the rich guy both getting shot."

"Ah."

"But Jesse has kids with a woman in Solipatria."

"Really."

He nods. "Vicki Martin. She cleaned rental units at motels in the morning after she took her kids to school. Then she clerked at the Circle K until it was time to pick them up in the afternoon."

"Am I hearing a past tense?"

"*Sí*, she was T-boned in her Subaru. A broken ankle and some ribs. Now she can't work and she has no car. She's getting kicked out of her trailer. The county might take the kids. Unless she gets some help. "

"And if somebody, ah, helped her, then she would get word to Jesse and he would be willing to talk?"

He nods and draws on the cigar. "This is what my cousin in the prison says."

"How much help?"

"Forty-eight hundred would get her caught up for a while is what my cousin heard."

"In cash of course."

"*De seguro.*"

"And is this something you can handle for me?

"Sorry. I must stay out of sight on this one."

"So I have to do it myself."

"Vickie's life is what you gringos call a shitstorm right now. It's not her fault."

"Fair point. How do I find this Vickie?"

"Del Sol trailer park, Space 13. Old green single-wide. Wrecked Subaru in the driveway."

He smokes, we contemplate the starlit night, and I realize I have all the answers I'm likely to get. Then he touches my thigh just below the hem of my shorts.

"I do have blankets and wine in the Jeep," I say.

He looks back at the dim silhouettes of my Jeep and No Trespassing sign in the moonlight. "Long way."

"What, it's only—"

But he's covering my mouth with a hungry kiss and spinning me around and bending me over the Harley and as usual with him I go from zero to sixty in ten seconds.

"That was expeditious," I say a short time later.

"The best ones are like that."

"Mm." I shrug. "I like having your weight on top of me sometimes, though. Like when the journey matters more than the destination?"

"Just remember, you asked for it."

"I think I can handle it."

We share a chuckle, he lights a joint, draws on it, and passes it over.

I take a puff and hand it back. We spend several minutes in companionable silence.

"Tell me more about this guy Barney," he says.

I brief him on what Lita and I dug up during our afternoon of combing through databases and even making a few plain old telephone calls—Barney's arrival in Palm Springs from Phoenix, his background in water rights and real estate, his passion for thoroughbreds, his estate in Mira Las Palmas.

He whistles. "Mira Las Palmas. Where rich people go to feel poor."

"Roger that," I say. "Anyway, he has a pretty clean record as an adult, but he was busted twice as a kid. The first time was for shoplifting a pint of Jack Daniels."

"Who could blame him?"

"And the other time was for loan-sharking."

"Loan sharking? A kid?"

"Yeah, in high school. He ran a trapline for a guy named Marco Gallegos," I say. "Including knuckle work, apparently."

"This Marco. A man who could make trouble disappear?"

"Somebody did. The case was dismissed two days after Barney got arrested."

"And as an adult?"

"An Arizona tax fraud case that settled out of court."

"And there's a daughter?"

"Uh-huh." I describe Skeeter and her visit to my place at the wheel of her father's SUV.

"We backgrounded her and it doesn't appear she's ever been much of anything but daddy's girl," I tell him. "Mother died of ovarian cancer when she was eight, no siblings, finished high school and two years of college, no job history to speak of. She lives in the pool house and is entirely dependent on him for financial support. She's on the payroll for his racehorse charity, but doesn't seem to do any actual work. Jamie says she mostly watches cop shows with her father."

Chapter Ten

WITH ALL THE FRESH ENDORPHINS sloshing around my system, I hope to sleep well, but no such luck. Thanks to the Jamie Lochner case, my mind's a hamster wheel.

And Duke's no help. A little after 4, he woofs me awake with his alert bark. A glance outside tells me motion detector lights in front are on. I join him at the window, but we see nothing unusual.

"Hey, buddy, your coyote pals sniffing around again?"

He scratches at the door to let me know he'd like to find out.

"All right, but make it quick," I tell him. "Mama needs her beauty sleep."

I let him out, watch as he sniffs the area in front of the house, then barks down the hill a few times, then returns to the door and looks down the hill like he wants me to join him for a moonlight ramble.

"Not tonight," I tell him. I lead him back to the bedroom, where he curls up on the floor with a reproachful look.

***

I'm at my groggiest when, 16-ounce Starbucks Americano in hand, I meet with Ike to plot our next move.

It's early and his office is quiet when I let myself in. I find Ike at Glenn's desk out front, working the Times crossword and watching a baseball game on the widescreen in the lobby. An info box on the screen says it's the bottom of the eighth and the Red Sox are beating the Tigers, 8-3.

Ditto steps out of his Amazon box, stalks over, sniffs my sneaker to see if I still smell like Duke, shoots me a glare from the one good eye, and returns to the box.

Ike is about a third of the way down the crossword, scrawling answers without pausing to think. He uses only the Across clues. If he needs a Down clue to solve the puzzle, he counts it a loss and moves on to the business section.

"Eleven-letter word for cat lover," he says as I take a chair in front of the desk.

"Schizophrenic?"

"That's thirteen letters, and Ditto assures me those studies are fake and cats do not cause schizophrenia."

"All the same to me. I'm a dog person."

"As Ditto knows so well," he says. "It's ailurophile."

"Who cares? A barista just called me ma'am." I wave the Americano at him.

"Thoughts and prayers, Dana." He clicks off the TV. "But to what do I owe the honor of this visit and why wouldn't you tell me on the phone?"

"It's a delicate situation. Remember you said not to work on the Jamie Lochner case other than backgrounding Barney and Nielle?"

"Uh-huh."

"Well, I got a call from my friend."

"Not the Chaplain."

Ike prefers to know as little as possible about the Chaplain so as to preserve deniability in case he blows up in our faces one day. But the information he brings us? That, Ike is fine with.

"In my defense," I say, "this particular call resulted from a feeler I put out before you told me to stop working on the case."

"All right, give it to me."

I tell him about the prison rumor in Solipatria.

"Jesus," he says. "Tony Alvarez hired a hitman?"

"He at least tried to, apparently."

Ike pulls a pencil from the cup on the desk and flips it in the air for several seconds, eyes focused somewhere over the horizon.

"Let me see if I have this right," he says at last. "We've got our client's lover and her husband both killed with her gun—let's stipulate for the sake of argument it actually was hers—while or just after she was with them, about which she denies all knowledge. And now there's a possible hitman in the mix."

"That's about the size of it."

"Do the police know about this supposed hitman?"

"Not according to my friend," I say. "Should we tell them?"

"Not until we know if he hurts or helps our client."

"Hurts her how?"

"I wish I knew." He sighs. "But I think this is on us, at least for now."

"Meaning I'm back in action?"

"Yep, start your meter. What do we know about this hitman?"

I lay it out in detail, starting with the rumor that Tony was looking for one and continuing through the $4,800 in cash for

Vicki Martin in Solipatria so she will contact Jesse Medina at the prison and clear him to tell us the name of Tony's hitman.

Ike drums his fingers on the desk. "Any chance we're being played by this guy Jesse and his woman?"

"Sure, if it was just us. But nobody down there is gonna play my friend."

"I'll get $4,800 from the safe here and you can go down and figure out if there's anything to this," he says. "You going today?"

"Can't think why not."

"All right," he says. "Let me get the cash and we'll head for the jail."

"The jail?"

"We need to talk to Jamie about this."

"Before we even know what's going on?"

"The look on her face when we ask her about the hitman may tell us exactly that."

Ten minutes later we pull into the parking lot at the police station and jail, Ike in his Maserati and me in my humble Jeep.

Out front there's a memorial to Frank as a slain officer, complete with a statue of him in full uniform. It looks enough like the husband I remember that I have to turn my head as we pass it.

"Still hurts, huh?" Ike asks."

"Always," I say.

"Want to grab a beer and talk after we do this?"

"Nope, but thanks."

Inside the jail, a 30-something guard with "Salinas" on her badge checks our IDs and Ike's briefcase, then takes us through a door fit for a bank vault. The power lock snaps shut behind us.

Salinas has a limp, two black eyes, and a purple bruise in the middle of her forehead.

"Inmate do that?" Ike asks as she escorts us down a long, echoing hallway with gray cinder block walls.

"Yeah," she says.

Ike hands her a business card. "Corrections doesn't treat you right, you give me a call, eh?"

She eyes the card, pockets it, mutters, "Maybe," and shows us into a conference room with more gray walls and a table bolted to the floor.

The room has a big dark window with one-way glass. Above it is a video camera and beside it is a poster that warns in large red print, "NO SMOKING. NO BEVERAGES. NO PHYSICAL CONTACT WITH INMATE. YOU ARE UNDER OBSERVATION." The place feels like the sign needs one more sentence: ABANDON ALL HOPE, YE WHO ENTER HERE.

When Salinas brings Jamie in and shackles her to the table, she's in a blue jumpsuit.

She still manages to look gorgeous. Blue is a good color for her, the blond mane is tied off in a ponytail, and she even has on a little makeup.

"When are you getting me out of here?" she hisses at Ike. "Between the guards and the dykes it's worse than high school."

"You're being arraigned tomorrow morning," Ike says. "With any luck, you'll be out on bail by the end of the week."

"I better," she says. "Otherwise, why did I have to give you a million-dollar retainer?"

"That's a bargain when rich people kill each other," Ike says. "We'll do what we can to get the charges dropped before trial. But Dana has come up with something we need to run by you. What do you know about this hitman that Tony was hiring to kill Barney?"

"What?"

"Yeah," I say. "Apparently Tony was working through somebody at the prison in Solipatria to find a hitman to kill your husband."

"A hitman?"

"We're still running it down," I say. "But that's how it looks."

Her face goes blank for a few seconds. Then it crumples into tears.

"Aw," she snuffles. "He loved me so much."

Ike looks as surprised as me. "What's love got to do with it?"

"He was trying to have Barney killed for me. It's so sweet."

"So you didn't know about this?" I ask.

"Of course not. How would I?"

***

Outside the jail, Ike and I climb into his Beamer for a post mortem.

"What's your radar say?" he asks as he switches on the AC. "Was she in on it?"

"No clue."

"Same here. I mean, we've got two guys apparently killed with our client's gun, one of whom may or may not have been trying to hire a hitman to kill the other one. WTF is going on with these people?"

"Maybe the answer's in Solipatria," I say.

Chapter Eleven

SOLIPATRIA is a weird little town.

For one thing, it's at the bottom of the Coachella Valley, where everything is weird. Not just the dying Salton Sea, but also the sprawling squatter camp of Slab City and the desert religious shrine known as Salvation Mountain.

Another thing about Solipatria: About half its residents are behind bars, because Solipatria State Correctional Center is inside the city limits. Throw in the thousand-plus people who work there, and it's fair to say over two-thirds of the population is doing time at Solipatria State one way or another.

Oh—and the place is 131 feet below sea level, making it the lowest city in the western hemisphere. It does have a 184-foot flagpole so the Solipatria Chamber of Commerce can boast it's not entirely under water.

I find Del Sol Mobile Estates on Railway Avenue at the east edge of Solipatria. It's about as depressing as you'd expect. Maybe forty spaces, a third of them empty, across the street from a rail line running atop a gravel levee. The sign at the entrance says the Del Sol Mobile Estates are "Cheap—Close—Convenient."

Close and convenient to what is not specified. But Vicki's green single-wide is on the corner closest to the railroad with all its noise and diesel fumes. I know this because of the mangled red Subaru Forester in the driveway where it was presumably dropped by the tow-truck after being T-boned.

I park on the street and walk up for a look at Space 13. The trailer is at least forty years old, maybe fifty. Sun-bleached green aluminum siding, a boxlike entryway of the same siding tacked onto the front, white plywood skirting, a ground-mounted satellite dish by the trailer hitch in front, and a humming air conditioner on one window. There's a yellow plastic kiddie picnic table beside an empty blue plastic kiddie pool in the weedy dirt yard.

A glance at the Subaru tells me Vicki is lucky to have survived the T-boning. The driver's door is bashed in at least a foot, the airbag is draped over the front seat, and the interior glitters with shards of window glass.

"I'm just glad the girls weren't in the car," comes a voice from the entryway of the trailer. "I was on my way back from dropping them off at school."

I turn to see an overweight 30-something with stringy brown shoulder-length hair and one of those permanent inverted smiles that people call a resting bitch face. Her left leg's on a four-wheeled knee walker and the foot is in a plastic boot. If her ribs are still bandaged from the crash, I can't see it because she's wearing a loose red top above her shorts and flip-flops.

"Hi," I say. "You Vicki Martin? I'm, ah, I've heard, ah, well, I may have something, ah, for you, I—"

"I know who you are and why you're here," she says. "Come in."

The inside of the trailer's a little nicer than the outside would suggest. The furnishings are old but clean. A rip in the orange vinyl sofa has been patched with duct-tape almost the same color as the vinyl.

"Catwalk Wars" plays from a wide-screen on the wall. The tall blond hostess, a helium-voiced anorexic with big fake boobs, is telling an aspiring designer, "I would totally wear your look to the Oscars."

Vicki clicks it off and sees me studying a set of photos on a chipped wooden dresser under the screen. They're lined up on either side of a small shrine to the Virgin of Guadalupe, complete with a flickering candle.

A photo next to the Virgin shows a younger and lighter Vickie perched on the back fender of a four-wheeler out in the desert with folded brown ridges in the background. The seat is occupied by a burly Latino with rattlesnake neck tattoos, a braided ponytail, and a mouth frown not unlike Vickie's.

I point. "That's Jesse?"

"Yep," she says. "*Mi cariño por siempre.*"

I check the impulse to advise her that *por siempre*—"for always"—only means until the night he doesn't come home, and turn my attention to the rest of the photos.

They show two little dark-haired girls, spaced about a year apart, at various stages of life. In the early pictures, they have the sweet, wide-eyed smiles that girls do before life starts happening to them. In the latest ones, they look to be ten or so. The smiles are more careful, the eyes a little narrower, like they're keeping their dreams to themselves now that Dad's not around anymore.

Vicki points at a picture of the younger one. "That's Annie," she says, then points at the other one. "And that's Emmy. They're my life. I don't know what I'd do without them."

My cop instincts kick in and I try for a welfare check.

"They're beautiful," I say. "Are they here now? I'd love to meet them."

"They're at school. Jesse's sister takes them since I can't drive."

Vickie trundles the knee walker over to the orange sofa, drops onto a cushion, and winces. She pops a capsule from a red and black ZaZa bottle on the chipped Formica coffee table and chases it with a long pull from a bottle of Mountain Dew.

"So," she says.

"I'm sure it's tough with Jesse in prison and then the car accident and all."

"You got no idea."

"So, um."

"Show me and I'll make the call while you listen," she says. "Then you can leave it and go."

I pull a Ziploc containing forty-eight one-hundred-dollar bills from my sling bag and fan the contents onto the coffee table next to a reverse harem romance novel. The cover depicts a blonde—not dissimilar to Jamie Lochner—snowed in with six male hunks.

"Mind if I count it?" Vickie says.

I shake my head.

She does, with remarkable speed and dexterity for a woman on ZaZa and whatever's in the Mountain Dew.

"Bring up your number on your phone." She holds out her hand.

"What? Why?"

"Jesse will call you."

"When?"

"When he can."

"How does he have a phone in prison?"

"He rents it from another inmate," Vickie says. "Two packages of ramen noodles per call."

I bring up the number and pass over my phone. Vickie lifts hers from the coffee table and taps in a number. She puts the phone on speaker as it rings.

"¿Sí?" a man mutters, almost too low to hear.

"Tell Jesse it's okay."

"Jesús?"

"Sí, Jesús." Vicki says. "Jesse."

"Bueno," the voice says. "And the number?"

Vicki reads my number off my phone screen. The man reads it back and the call drops. She sweeps the hundreds back into the Ziploc.

I look at the money, then Vickie. "Um."

"What?"

"It's a lot of money."

"Yeah?"

"Is Jesse gonna call?"

"Don't worry, he'll call."

Back in the Jeep, I start the engine, crank up the AC against 90 degrees of hot, and lower the windows to cool off the interior.

Then I wait.

For what, I'm not sure. Lack of a better idea, maybe. Or perhaps because maybe we are being played and I don't want to get too far from Ike's $4,800 till I hear from Jesse. Vickie comes to the window of the trailer and shoots me a glare. Her expression says she'd be wearing a frown even if it wasn't built in.

She comes to the door of the entryway on her knee walker. I turn off the AC to hear better. She says, "Well?"

"Well, he didn't call."

"He will," Vickie says. "Now get out of my yard. Neither one of us needs for you to be seen here."

She's right. I raise the windows and put the Jeep in reverse.

An hour later, I'm few miles north of the Salton Sea, passing through a wide spot in the road called Mecca, when my phone chimes and a strange number comes up on the screen.

"You want a *moreno* name of Efren Mendoza," says a voice I don't recognize. "He deals out of the Rattlesnake in Caliente Springs. You got that? Efren Mendoza. *El moreno.*"

"Yeah, but what's a—"

Then he's gone and I'm thinking, of course a full-time dealer and part-time hitman would hang out at the Rattlesnake. They keep a diamondback in a class cage behind the bar at the Rattlesnake. But what's a *moreno*?

I bring up Ike's cell number on the phone and tap it to life.

"Dana," he says. "You find—"

"What's a *moreno*?"

"I don't—wait, yeah, I've heard that before, a, ah, a really dark-complected guy I think."

"Then that's what we're looking for. A dark-skinned guy named Efren Mendoza who deals out of the Rattlesnake in Caliente Springs. Also known as *el moreno* apparently."

"Jesus," Ike says. "That's it for forty-eight hundred dollars?"

"That's it. So now I poke around a little, right?"

"You kidding? No way."

"Sure," I tell him. "Gringo lady hits The Rattlesnake in the middle of the day, orders a Moscow mule, who's gonna notice?"

"Just get up here and let's talk this out."

Chapter Twelve

"SO IT'S AVILA AND JEFFERSON then?" Ike says from across the desk.

It's an hour and a half later and we're sipping iced lemon water in the air-conditioned hush of his office. I've briefed him on the call from Jesse on the rented prison cell phone and we've thrashed through all of the options. All except the one I'm reluctant to bring up. I know it will make Ike nervous.

"Sure, we could call Gary," I say. "Or I could—"

He's stopped me with a raised hand. "I said no poking around. Not with this guy. We're going to Avila."

"But Jamie's gun killed Tony and Barney both and—"

"Allegedly."

"All right, allegedly killed them both," I say. "But what if she really was in on it and we go to Avila? Aren't we incriminating our own client?"

"Well, hell."

"Smart people always miss the obvious. Can you think of anything else obvious you're missing?"

"Wha—oh. Jamie could be next."

"Yeah, 'cause we got no idea what's really going on here except everybody who touches it turns up dead. So...the Chaplain?"

"I don't see a way around it," Ike says with a shake of his head. "Forty-eight hours, then I go to Avila and Jefferson. And we never had this conversation."

I start for the door.

"And you stay out of it," Ike tells my back. "Let him do what he does."

"Absolutely," I say.

From the Jeep, I shoot a phone picture of Ike's parking lot and send another "beautiful day in the desert" message on Cinder. When will the Chaplain call? There's no telling. I just hope it's before Ike drags me into a meeting with Gary Avila and Ray Jefferson.

My phone lights up almost at once. "I could use your help."

"*Sí?*"

"*Sí.*" And I tell him about my visit to Solipatria and my chat with Jesse, and about the *moreno* Efren Mendoza who reportedly hangs out at the Rattlesnake in Caliente Springs.

"*Bueno,*" he says. "But it could take a while. I don't know many people up there."

"I've only got forty-eight hours, then Ike's taking it to Gary Avila. Whatever this is, I want to stay ahead of Gary on it."

"I'll see what I can do."

"When you find him, I want to talk to him."

"No good," he says. "Too dangerous."

"I'll wait while you get him ready."

Long pause.

"You'll do what I say?"

"Don't I always?"

He taps off without answering. But I think I hear a chuckle.

Once I'm home, I call Lita and set her to work on Efren Mendoza's back trail. Then I put together a tuna and cheese sandwich, cut it into two identical triangles because sometimes I need things to be just so, add a side of kale chips and carry it out to the patio. There I take refuge from the sun at a table in the shade of a big umbrella and do a news cruise on my laptop while I eat my lunch.

Today the news people, not to mention social media, are aflame over a professional panhandler so gorgeous that one Instagram scroll goblin wants to sign him up as a model.

But it's not just his looks that make Sean Steele—not a government name, I'm guessing—celebrity of the moment.

It's also that he makes over two hundred bucks a day panhandling along Palm Canyon Drive with a brown cardboard sign reading "Please Help."

And that he has better than 25,000 TikTok followers and of course a link so they can donate by phone app.

And that he has no desire to change. As he puts it when a TV reporter tracks him down, "Don't hate on me, but some people just don't need a real job and I'm happy to be one of them."

I'm crunching a kale chip and trying to imagine how life could get any less fair when I smell Partagas smoke. A familiar voice says, "You know kale doesn't make you live longer. It just seems longer."

I look up, and there's Imaginary Frank across the table, the same old grin on his face. The real Frank hated kale. He called it the leaf of Satan. Wouldn't eat it in any form, chips or otherwise. So I ate it to spite him. And still do,

"You need a haircut," I tell him. Which is the same thing I told him the morning he got shot.

Today he's in his jogging outfit—gray shorts, Adidas running shoes, and the Springsteen T-shirt that says "The Only Boss I Listen To." It still hangs in his closet, still smells like him, and hasn't been touched since he died.

"You had good legs and not much gut for a guy your age," I tell him.

"You had good everything. Still do."

"Not good enough to keep you from screwing around and having a couple of outside kids, you bastard."

"Guilty as charged," he says. "But don't you need to put that in the rearview? For your own good?"

"I do. But I can't. Not yet."

"How are they? My kids?"

"Thriving. But shut up or I'll start crying."

He draws on the Partagas for a long time with a reflective look in his eyes. Then he cocks his head. "Jamie hired you about ten days ago, right?"

"Uh-huh."

"And Barney showed up with Nielle a few hours later?"

"Yeah, but—"

"And you tracked Tony down at Manny's the next day?"

"Yes, Wednesday morning."

"And he was killed early Thursday morning."

"Yeah, but where you going with this?"

"One day after you found him."

Now I'm silent for a while. Then, "Huh."

"You should listen to Duke, he says."

"What?"

"You want to figure this out, you have to listen to Duke."

"Duke doesn't talk."

Duke is on the flagstones beside my chair. He can't hear Imaginary Frank, of course, but he hears me say his name. His ears perk up and he lifts his head with the hopeful look that says "Fetch?"

"He talks," Imaginary Frank says. "You just don't listen."

"What does that mean?"

"How would I know? I only know what you know. You know that."

"Stop talking in circles."

Which is a pointless remark. Imaginary Frank is nothing more than the voice of my subconscious, so of course he doesn't know anything that I don't. But he seems so real.

"Gotta run," he says. He rises and jogs across the patio. When he reaches the edge, he looks back and says "Loveya, baby."

He flicks the Partagas into the sand and vanishes into the brush.

"You, too," I whisper.

Duke bumps my knee and gives me Fetch eyes again.

"Yeah, yeah, buddy, hang on." I get one of his tennis balls from the deck box and throw it after Imaginary Frank. Duke vanishes for a few seconds, then comes back with the ball, mucky with sand and slobber.

I pick it up with three fingers—the minimum you can use and still throw a ball—and toss it again.

Finally he tires of it, drops the ball by the deck box, trots over to the table, and fixes his gaze on my plate.

I set it on a flagstone and watch as he inhales the bread crusts I saved for him. But the four kale chips? He sniffs them once and gives me the side-eye.

"Just like your master," I tell him.

He ignores me and wanders off toward the Jeep parked in the driveway.

I take the plate in and rinse it off, then decide on a nap. I don't want Duke running loose while I'm asleep , so I go to the front door, put two fingers between my teeth and give him the "come-in" whistle.

He pokes his head out from behind the Jeep and gives me another side-eye.

"*Hier!*" I say.

"*Hier*" is German because that's the language Duke, like most police dogs, was trained in. It's K-9 for "Come!" but he still doesn't.

Which is a serious breach of protocol.

I'm halfway to the Jeep to straighten him out when Imaginary Frank's line goes off in my head like an IED: "Duke talks, you just don't listen."

I sprint the rest of the way and see when I reach him that he's doing what he's been doing ever since the Lochners showed up a week ago: sniffing around the rear of the Jeep where Nielle Lochner stood and smoked her cigarillo.

I drop to my knees and grope under the bumper. Moments later, I'm holding in my hand the proof of my own stupidity for not listening to Duke sooner: the little square magnetic tracking device that Nielle clipped to the frame of the Jeep while I was in the SUV with Barney.

The same kind of tracker you can get from Amazon for less than ten bucks. The same kind of tracker that that works over the cell network to let you locate whoever you planted it on anywhere in the world, with nobody the wiser.

Nobody except Duke. He sniffs the tracker and looks at me. No judgment, just a dog's usual plea for affirmation.

"Good boy!" I tell him. "Go-o-o-o-d boy!"

There's no official K-9 command for that, so I use English. But Duke gets the message, especially when I scratch his rump and say it a couple more times. He gives me a tongue-out smile and closes his eyes in bliss.

Chapter Thirteen

I PARK MYSELF in an Adirondack chair on the patio, close my eyes, and backtrack through the days since Barney and Nielle showed up in my driveway right after Jamie did. The days since Nielle put a tracker on my Jeep.

The first question is, how did they find me? Another IED goes off in my head. Barney knew enough about Jamie and Tony to get Tony fired. And he knew enough about trackers to have his daughter put one on my car. He must have been tracking Jamie's Mercedes when she came to my place to hire me.

But so what if she came to some random house in the foothills? Did Barney think she and Tony had found a new nest and were back in business?

If so, the visit would have disabused him of that notion. Besides, he already knew when he got here that I'm a private investigator, what with his phony request for help finding out who was embezzling his racehorse charity.

So what was the point of the visit? The only possible reason was to plant a tracker on my car.

But why?

Jamie claimed right from the start that Barney and Nielle killed Tony. And Imaginary Frank had pointed out that he was killed one day after I found him. Did Barney figure out that my stop at Manny's meant I had found Tony, then have Nielle go down there and kill him?

But again, why? Barney had gotten Tony fired and Tony had dumped Jamie and left town. Why kill him when everything seemed to be working out as planned? Especially since Barney had to know that his scene with Bish and his demand that Tony be fired would land him at the top of the list of suspects once Tony turned up dead.

So what would Barney's angle be in killing Tony? It made no sense.

And, yet, and yet, and yet—he'd had his daughter put a tracker on my car and Tony was killed the day after I found him. If Jamie didn't do it, it had to have happened just before she showed up, at which time Barney was asleep sixty miles north in his mansion in Palm Springs.

But Tony was to all evidence killed with Jamie's Ruger, as was Barney. How could that happen? I can think of only two people who might know: Jamie and Nielle Lochner. Luckily, Jamie's out on bail now, to the tune of another million bucks.

In half an hour, I'm at her door at the Parsons.

She greets me with a frown. "You."

"I need to look at your car."

"What? Why?"

"Just trust me. Where is it?"

"I don't know. They valet here."

"Ask them to bring it around, will you?"

"Why?"

"Just do it. I'll explain while they're getting it."

She makes the call on the room phone.

"So. What?"

I tell her about finding the tracker on my Jeep with a little help from Duke, and why it could only have been put there by Nielle while Barney was faking an attempt to hire me.

"Jesus," she says. "Why would he do that?"

"The only way Barney would know about me, much less care," I say, "is if he knew you came to see me, and the only way he would know that is if he was tracking you. So we need to check your car for a tracker."

She picks up the room phone. "Where the hell is my car? Uh-huh, uh-huh? Well, hurry."

She hangs up. "But why would he want to track you?"

"There's only one reason I can think of. When he saw on the tracker that you come up here, he did an Internet search on my address—"

"That would have been Skeeter," she says. "She's the computer nerd. The Internet and watching cop shows with Barney is her whole life. Or was, but now. . ."

"Whatever. But they found out Jacinto Investigations was at my address and then it was an easy guess why you'd be talking to a private investigator."

"They knew I was trying to find Tony!" She pales as she works it out. "Oh, shit. And you did find him the next day at Manny's, so the day after that he, oh, God, Barney went down there and shot Tony with my gun right before I got there so the police would think it was me."

"Except he didn't," I say. "Remember what Jefferson and Avila said? Zero evidence that Barney left the property that morning. Or Nielle, for that matter."

"They have to be wrong. Who else could it be?"

"Well, you obviously."

"Is that what you think?"

"Not me," I say. "But Ike's wondering."

"Oh, God. I'll get a new lawyer."

"Don't bother. Another lawyer would have the same questions as Ike, but not be as good. A lawyer has to give his client the same defense, regardless what he thinks of her guilt or innocence, as long as he doesn't lie to the court or let her do it."

"But you don't think I did it."

"It's more of a feeling than anything thought-out," I say. "When you came to my house, I resented everything about you. Your looks, your money, your luck. And I kind of still do. But you know what?"

"What?"

"You just don't act guilty. You left a trail of evidence a mile wide, you make admissions against your own interest and...anyway, when you're a cop as long as I was, and you're also married to one, you learn to trust your gut. And mine says you didn't kill anybody. Either that or you're the greatest actress since Marilyn Monroe. Or you're completely insane."

She smiles a little at that. "Thanks. But if it wasn't me, who killed Tony and how did they get hold of my gun?"

"Not to mention who killed Barney?" I say. "And there's only one person who can answer any of these questions."

***

"Why didn't the police find it when they had my car?" Jamie nods at the tracker I found under her rear bumper when the valet pulled her Mercedes up to the door of the Parsons. The tracker is now rattling in the cup-holder as we rocket up Palm Canyon Drive with "All You Ever Do Is Bring Me Down" blasting from the audio system. Duke is doing his best to get comfortable in what passes for the back seat of a Mercedes convertible.

I shrug. "They were looking for blood, fingerprint, and firearms evidence. I might have missed a tracker myself, under the circumstances."

"You think she's tracking us now?" Jamie asks.

"Almost certainly. You can set an alert on those things for whenever the car moves. And slow down. The last thing we need is a police stop. Avila would be here in five minutes."

"They can do that?"

"They can and they do. You're only the most famous murder suspect on the West Coast right now. The officer's screen will light up like World War III the second he types in your license number."

"I'm only doing sixty."

"The speed limit is thirty."

"Really?"

But she does hit the brakes. Soon we're down to forty.

"Is this even legal?" she asks. "Will I go back to jail for harassing Skeeter if I go in there?"

"The defense has every right to interview a prosecution witness," I shout over the music. "If she'll talk to us."

"Why would she?"

"The average criminal freaks out when a cop shows up at the house. They tell themselves not to talk, then they do anyway."

"But you're not a cop."

"I was a cop, which Skeeter knows if she backgrounded me."

"Which she undoubtedly did," Jamie says.

"Can you turn that off?"

"Sorry, I needed a dose of home." She taps the audio screen and the music stops with one final "I expected way too much of you."

"I'm also a private investigator," I continue. "She knows that, too, and it's another pressurizer. Plus, I'm with you."

"She hates me."

"Exactly," I say. "So she'll talk to us if we can get in. And she knows we're coming if she's tracking us."

"Which she absolutely will be doing."

"So how does the gate work?"

"It opens when the system reads that." She points at a UFH tag in the corner of the windshield.

"Unless Skeeter canceled it."

"Oh, right."

"Or she's watching us on the gate camera and blocks us?"

"Yeah, I think she can do that," she says.

"Fifty bucks says she lets us in and at least comes out to scream at us when we pull up to the mansion."

"I don't think she'll be up there, not with Daddy's ghost still roaming the halls," she says. "Probably still in the pool house."

"All right, when we pull up to the pool house."

We reach the gate and stop. Nothing happens. We sit there. More nothing. I'm thinking I would have lost my fifty bucks to the millionaire in the driver's seat if she had taken the bet.

"I think I can climb over it," she says. "You wanna?"

No way am I saying 'no way' to this twenty-something with her BMI of 22. So I'm about to force out an insincere 'of course' when the two halves of the gate screech back.

"Told ya," I say as we roll through.

Ahead of us is a circular palm-lined drive that leads up to a parking terrace below the mansion.

But Jamie takes a single-lane drive leading off to the right. It winds around the towering adobe walls of the mansion, past tennis courts, and then to an adobe pool house with a parking spot in back.

A parking spot occupied by the same black SUV that Nielle drove to my place the day she planted the tracker on my car.

Behind the pool house, two gardeners are using a ladder to throw withered brown palm fronds over the back wall. Beyond the wall, desert ridges studded with yucca and ocotillo and laced with hiking trails rise up toward the slopes of the San Jacintos.

Jamie stops behind the SUV. "Do we knock on the door or wait her out?"

"Let's wait a little."

Time passes. Jamie taps the audio screen and the music picks up with "I think I saw it coming from the start."

Nielle's face appears at a window for a few seconds, then disappears. The door opens a crack and one eye peers out. The door closes. Finally Nielle steps out in the brown glasses.

Jamie lowers her window. "Hello, Skeeter."

"Don't call me that."

"Oh, yeah," Jamie says. "I forgot. Only Daddy was allowed to call you that. Hello, Nielle."

"Hello, slut."

"At least I had something he wanted," Jamie says. "Unlike you."

"Shut up, slut. He loved me more."

"Keep telling yourself that."

I grab the trackers from the cupholder and step out of the Mercedes. Duke jumps out behind me, tests the air, and focuses on Nielle. His ears are at full attention and his eyes are wide in his patented scary police dog stare.

"Hello, Skeeter," I say. "I'm here to interview you for the defense."

"I'm not saying anything."

"Your choice." I hold out the trackers. "But I believe these are yours." I pause for a two-count. "Skeeter."

"You don't call me that either. And I never saw those before in my life."

Jamie steps out of the Mercedes and leans on a front fender.

I let Duke sniff the trackers, then wave him forward. He advances to within a couple feet of Nielle.

"Duke here says otherwise." Now I wait a four count. "You put one on my car the day you and Barney came to visit."

"No, I didn't."

"Duke says you did. He saw you do it and he's been sniffing around the spot where you stood ever since."

"I said I'm not talking."

"And you put one on Jamie's car, too, didn't you? That's how you followed her to my house. And then you tracked me to Riviera Dunes and went down there the next day and killed Tony with Jamie's gun to frame her, didn't you?"

"You know I didn't. I was right here on the property when that happened. That slut killed him, just like she killed my daddy."

"We both know that's not true. You stole that gun from her console and somehow killed Tony with it to hurt Jamie and then you killed your father with it because you knew he loved her more than you. I'm just glad you didn't find a way to finish Jamie off, too. That had to be part of the plan, right?"

"You shut up about my daddy and he...you don't know...he...his...you shut up." She takes off the glasses and knuckles away tears.

Suddenly, I remember the night Duke tried to tell me someone was prowling around outside. "And you came back to get your tracker, didn't you? Except my dog scared you off. What I'm wondering is, why didn't you retrieve the one on Jamie's car? Cops impound it before you got the chance?"

Jamie speaks up. "Can I ask her a question?"

"What question?"

She whispers in my ear.

"Jesus Christ," I say. "Really?"

"I just realized."

"Go for it."

"Look, Nielle," Jamie says. "I know we've had our differences."

Nielle puts the glasses back on.

"And I'm sorry I called you Skeeter. I know you loved your father and he loved you."

Nielle's face says she's not buying it. But she is listening.

"So could I ask you one question?"

"What?"

"Remember when you saw the police dog sniff out my gun and the officers dig it up? Remember how you said that on TV for the whole world to see?"

"Yeah?"

"How did you know the gun was mine?"

"What? I—"

"You never saw that gun. Your father and I bought it at a gun shop in Thousand Palms. After that it never left my console except when he taught me to shoot it out by Joshua Tree or later on when I practiced with it in the basement every couple of months. So how did you know it was my gun?"

"It...I...it must have been lying around the mansion at some point."

Jamie crosses her arms and does a pretty good imitation of Duke's suspect stare. "That gun was either in my purse or my hand any time it was in the mansion. So how did you know it was mine when the police found it?"

"It...I...Daddy must have told me what it looked like. I think he showed me a brochure after he bought it for you."

"Bullshit," I say. "You're lying through your teeth and we're going to tell the police and they'll figure out how and why you killed Tony and your father."

"She really never saw that gun of yours?" I ask as we pull away from a stunned Nielle.

"Nope, never."

"Well, that was brilliant. You ever want a real job, I've got work for you. With that brain and those looks, you'd kill."

"If you and Ike get me off, I get another three million per the prenup and half the estate in the will. I'll never have to work again and I don't intend to. I'm gonna go back to Texas and find Darren."

"If Nielle did kill Barney, maybe Ike could get the will overturned. You might get it all."

She beams. "Excellent. That's another seven or eight million, according to Zillow."

"Detail oriented, are we?"

"I keep track of things, yeah."

"Except everything we said back there was pure bullshit," I say. "There's exactly zero evidence either one of them killed Tony. It's just not possible. Yet somehow, the same gun killed Barney. Plus, do you really think Nielle would kill her father? Whatever else you can say about her, that girl really loved her Daddy."

"You know what Aunt Blue used to say? Love and hate is just flip sides of the same cowpie."

I have to chuckle. "I've heard that before, just not in those exact words. But, yeah, an old, old story."

Chapter Fourteen

I'M CALLING DUKE IN from his last outing of the day when my phone lights up with a strange number.

"I found your hitman," the Chaplain says. "Meet me at the windmills."

"You found—"

Too late, he's gone.

When I pull up to the No Trespassing sign at the wind farm, there's no Harley in sight. I cut my lights to wait, then see the briefest flare of what could be a kitchen match fifty yards out into the darkness.

I pull around the sign and nose the Jeep though the sand and mesquite towards what I hope is the right spot. I see the glow of a cigar tip in the darkness and moments later pull up beside the Chaplain's Harley.

There's enough moonlight that I can see he's leaning on the saddle. I get out and lean against the fender of the Jeep. "You found him?"

He nods. "His house. I went in the Rattlesnake around midnight and the bartender turned out to be someone I knew well at one time. She told me—"

"She?"

"*Sí*, Cristal. She told me—"

"How well?"

He chuckles a little. "Not as well as you."

"And this was when?"

"*Tiempos perdidos*," he says.

"Lost times."

He nods "When I came back from Afghanistan I was using. I cleaned up, but she didn't. I couldn't be around that, so I ended it. I heard she was dead."

"But she's not."

"No, but she's still using. She asked me if I wanted to hang out later. I told her the answer is still no."

"Huh."

"Now do you want to know about Efren?

"*Sí.*"

"She knows him as a dealer," he says. "Not a hitman."

"There's never a hitman. It's always just some loser who's hard up for cash."

"*Verdad*, Cristal said Efren will take any job that comes along. Apparently he shorted his suppliers. They want their money."

"As suppliers are wont to do."

"*Verdad*," he says. "Cristal says he's in the Rattlesnake every two or three days doing business."

"Is he there now?"

"Not for a day or two."

"Huh."

"But Cristal told me where he lives. She goes there herself sometimes."

"Really."

"I got the idea she doesn't always pay with money."

"Ah. And this address is in Caliente Springs?"

"Belinda Avenue, north side, two houses west of Del Norte."

"No address?"

"Just a description," he says. "But I went past. Old white clapboard, small, a shrine to the Virgin Mary in front."

I start to look for the spot on my map app, but he grabs my wrist.

"Turn that off and put it in the console."

I comply and he hands me a cheap burner phone like the ones he uses. "Take this. When we're done, I'll bury it with mine."

I nod.

Then he passes over a black ballcap from the Harley's saddlebag. I pull it down over my ash-blond shag and tuck the stray ends out of sight.

"You sure you're okay with this?" I ask him. "This guy did twenty-eight months in Solipatria for armed robbery and attempted murder, according to what Lita dug up. And there's a warrant out on him now for dealing."

The Chaplain pulls back the flap of his vest and I see the gleam of a pistol grip in his belt.

"Really? You never carry a gun, just the hammer."

"I have that, too." He pats the other flap.

"So how do we do this?"

***

A half hour later, I'm parked in deep darkness at the corner of Del Norte and Belinda, as instructed. Headlights off, burner in the console, both feet planted on the floor well clear of the pedals so the brake lights don't come on. I'm slumped down in the seat so the Chaplain's black ballcap doesn't show above the headrest.

Two lots ahead on the right a shrine to the Virgin stands under the dim glow of a streetlight. There's the Virgin herself, with three children kneeling in front of her. The windows of the little white house behind her are dark, and the driveway is empty. If I see lights or activity at the house, I'm to pull away and call the Chaplain.

Several boring minutes pass. Then a car with a loud muffler comes up Belinda. I shrink farther down in the seat as the headlights hit the interior of the Jeep, then fade as it continues past.

More boring minutes tick by. No action, no lights. A tap on the passenger window jolts me upright. The Chaplain has coasted in behind me with his headlight and engine off, and I've heard nothing. He nods, I nod, he slips up Del Norte, and vanishes into the shadows of the alley that runs behind the houses along Belinda.

Including *el moreno's* house.

I hold the burner between my knees under the dash and bring up the clock. It's 2:09 am. Also as instructed, I set a fifteen-minute timer and hide the phone in the console.

If he isn't back and hasn't called when the timer goes off, I'm to leave, bury the burner in the desert, call the Coachella County Sheriff's Office anonymous tip line and report somebody was just killed at the house on Belinda.

Before I have time to shrink down in the seat again, a little kid pedals past on a bicycle. No light except from the phone held to his ear. He doesn't spot me and continues on his way. But what he is doing out at two o'clock in the morning? He can't be ten years old. Where's his mother?

More waiting, but not boring now. Tense.

Was that a flicker of light in the house? Maybe a phone screen or flashlight? Or maybe just nerves. Why is this taking so long? To hell with the instructions. I'm getting my Glock out of the console and reaching for the doorhandle when the lights in the front room flash once. Then the burner chimes. I fish it out of the console and tap it to life.

"Get in here," the Chaplain says. "Come up the alley and use the back door."

***

"You did this? I didn't hear a shot."

"Not me." The Chaplain nudges the bare left foot of the dark-skinned dead man on the floor before us. "He's already stiff."

"That looks like Efren, all right."

"*Sí*. I found some ID in the bedroom. Also a Glock 38 in the nightstand, and a couple hundred in cash.

"No drugs?"

"Who knows?" the Chaplain says. "This is a crime scene. I'm not doing a real search and perhaps destroy evidence or leave some behind. I'm pushing it just being here.'

We're in a tiny screened-in porch at the back of the house. Efren's on his back, his torso in the kitchen, his legs blocking the doorway into the house. There's a bloody spot in the front of his T-shirt and a bullet hole in the middle of it surrounded by a circle of gunpowder residue. The bloody spot's not that big, meaning Efren's heart stopped pumping pretty soon after the bullet arrived. Judging from the size of the hole and powder residue around it, the shot came from a pretty big weapon. A .357 or a .45 maybe.

I squat for a closer look in the light from a single bare bulb in the porch ceiling. Besides the Adidas t-shirt, Efren's wearing cargo shorts. On his right arm a tattoo that reads "Every moment is a new beginning"—in English—spirals down to his knuckles through a tangle of roses. And he has an intricate neck tattoo of what might be intertwined rattlesnakes.

He's slight and dark-skinned, so much so that he looks more Ethiopian than Latino. But that happens in a melting pot like Southern California. He's also young—not much past 20, I'm guessing—and baby-faced.

"This guy is a hitman?" I ask the Chaplain. "And a dealer? He could be the kid I bought my Americano from this morning."

"You can't tell by how they look," he says. "But somebody did want him dead."

"Somebody who knew to come to the back door. And he left his shoes and gun in the bedroom."

"Somebody he was expecting."

"A customer?" I say. "Except wouldn't a user take the money too? And the Glock. A Glock's gotta be worth something on the street."

"Two, three hundred, maybe."

"So, apparently not a robbery."

He shrugs. "Maybe somebody he owed money?"

"His supplier?"

"Who knows?"

"What now?"

"You give me your burner and we get out of here and I bury it, and mine. Then I call my handler at Palm Springs Public Safety."

"Why would you—oh, Cristal."

"Sí. She won't last long when the police come to the Rattlesnake."

"And if she cracks, they find out about you."

"*Sí.* So my handler must hear it from me first."

"And he'll pass it along to the sheriff's office? The county has jurisdiction in Caliente Springs, not the Palm Springs police."

"*Sí.*"

"Will you be okay?"

"I think so," he says. "That shot didn't come from my gun."

"And me?"

"I won't mention you. And Cristal doesn't know about you."

I study him for a moment. "Thank you, *cariño.*"

"It's nothing," he says.

Chapter Fifteen

WAY TOO EARLY the next morning, Ike and I are at it again in his office. I've filled him in on what the Chaplain and I found on Belinda Avenue. Now we're trying to figure out what it means.

If anything.

"Just to confirm," I say. "Jamie's in the clear on this one, right?"

"I think, yeah," Ike says. "If the drug-dealer guy was killed, what, somewhere between two and twenty-four hours before you found him—"

"That's how I read it. He was stiff and rigor mortis starts a couple hours after death and lasts about a day," I say. "And Jamie was—"

"Safely tucked away at the Parsons except for the visit to Nielle's pool house in your custody," Ike says. "I'll check with security to make sure, but she's been a good little girl since I bailed her out. So who killed Efren?"

"Maybe nobody we know. Judging from the entry wound and the pattern of gunshot residue, it was probably a bigger gun than the .22 used on Tony and Barney. And one shot, not three."

"So unrelated?"

We give it a think.

Finally Ike speaks. "The simplest explanation would be that Efren's death is, in fact, unrelated to our client and her situation. Maybe he was shorting his suppliers, maybe a customer decided to stick him up, who knows? But chickens coming home to roost for a guy in a risky business is the simplest explanation. Just not our chickens."

"What does your gut say?"

"No way it's unrelated. Tony was looking for a hitman and he was put in touch with Efren and now he's the third body to turn up who's connected to the people in this case. Too many coincidences."

"But we've got no duty to report it to the police, right?"

"Only to our client."

Jamie greets us at the door to her suite at the Parsons in a hair band and a terry cloth bathrobe with a big gold P embroidered over the right breast.

"Will this take long?" she says. "My masseuse will be here any minute."

"Not long," Ike says. "And it's important."

She waves the glass of white wine in her hand at a bottle of Louis Jadot on the breakfast bar. "Help yourselves. We can talk on the patio."

She pulls back the drapes and slides open the glass doors. The patio not only overlooks the pool, but also has a fire pit. As she observed the day I met her, life's not bad behind the velvet rope.

Ike and I skip the Louis Jadot and follow her out to a table. It's pleasant, early enough in the day that the temperature is still under 80.

"As I indicated on the phone," Ike says when we're seated, "there's been what looks like a major development in your case."

"They caught whoever killed Barney and Tony? Are they dropping the charges? Can I get out of here? Who was it?"

"Maybe this guy." I bring up my phone and show her Efren's mug shot from an old burglary arrest in Indio. "Ever seen him?"

She studies the picture and shrugs. "Never. Who is he?"

"Efren Mendoza," Ike says. "Also known as *el moreno*. Either name mean anything to you?"

"Nope. Did he kill them?"

"Possibly. Dana tracked down the hitman that Tony supposedly hired to kill Barney and it turned out to be Mr. Mendoza."

Jamie turns an admiring look on me. "Seriously."

"I had some help from a friend, but, yeah."

"And they arrested him?"

"Not exactly," I say. "It turns out he's dead."

"What?"

"Somebody shot him."

"Within the last day or two," Ike says.

"I was in this room or at the pool that whole time except when Dana and I went down to see Skeeter," she says. "Just ask the maids. Or room service. Or security."

"I did," Ike says. "And by the way, nice catch on asking Nielle how she knew it was your gun the police found. Dana briefed me on that. Do you have a theory?"

Jamie shakes her head. "Nope, total mystery."

Ike sighs. "It's possible it doesn't mean anything, I suppose. Maybe Nielle was just guessing."

"Whatever," Jamie says. "But you know I didn't shoot your hitman, right?"

"We do," Ike says. "But—"

"So who did?"

"Good question," Ike says. "You have any ideas?"

"Ideas?" she says. "For the million dollars I gave you, isn't it your job to have ideas about how to nail Skeeter and get me off so I can enjoy Barney's money in peace?"

"That's exactly what we're trying to do," Ike tells her. "And if we can get the charges dropped, you'll get most of your retainer back, not to mention the bail. So work with us, okay?"

"Whatever."

***

"She's either really good or really innocent," I say as we cross the hotel lobby.

"I incline toward really good," Ike says. "I think I'm defending a guilty client."

"I thought that didn't matter."

"Legally and ethically, it doesn't. It's my duty to provide her with a vigorous defense regardless, as long as I don't let her lie to the court or do so myself."

"But?"

"But practically and morally, it does matter. A lot. Practically, I don't want to be blindsided if the police come up with some bombshell evidence at the last moment."

"And morally?"

"I have to know," he says. "I just have to know."

"Same here. But what do we do now?"

"We wait to see if the police tie Mendoza's death to our case."

"Or I could poke around a little."

"I didn't hear that."

Chapter Sixteen

PRETTY MUCH every law enforcement agency I ever heard of had its own Rain Man, a clerk in the Records Division who is invaluable because of his eidetic memory and his eye for pattern where the rest of us see nothing but random dots.

In the case of the Coachella County Sheriff's Department, the Rain Man is Louis Ballard. I worked with him for two decades at the Brawley sheriff's station, then Frank got killed and I hung out my shingle as a private investigator in Palm Springs. We haven't seen much of each other since then, but today I need his help.

The problem is that what I need from him is nothing I can call him about on his landline at work. I can't have it overheard, by, say, Sergeant Ray Jefferson, who would instantly pass it along to Lieutenant Gary Avila, who would instantly realize it's connected to his investigation of Barney Lochner's murder in Palm Springs.

And I can't call him on his cell, because he doesn't own one. Louis has a pathological fear of electromagnetic emissions and will not touch a cell phone, much less converse on one.

I call Louis's partner, Ernetta, who confirms that he's working today and she'll be picking him up at the Brawley when he gets off at five. They should be back home in Slab City by six, she says, and Louis should be finished with his after-work nap by seven.

I have a drive of two and a half hours ahead of me, so at three o'clock I load a Styrofoam cooler into the back of the Jeep and start down the west shore of the Salton Sea in 95 degrees of heat.

My first stop is 80-something miles later in Westmoreland, at the south end of the Salton. I pull into a Chevron station and pick up two bags of crushed ice.

I dump both bags into the cooler, then cross Route 78 to my real reason for stopping in Westmoreland: Salton Date Shakes.

A date shake is a giant milk shake with dates and honey thrown in, and it's like heroin for the stomach. Just one is reputed to add over a thousand calories to the waistline. I say reputed because I've never dared look it up. I just avoid date shakes when it's possible, and enjoy them when it's not.

Today it's not, because date shakes are the key to Louis's cooperation.

I buy three of them from a bubbly Latina teenager who, bless her heart, calls me *señorita* instead of *señora*. I give her a huge tip, take the shakes out to the Jeep and nestle the big cups in the ice of the cooler. It's another half hour to Louis's tank in the Slabs, and I can't let his shake turn to soup.

Louis's tank stored water before Slab City was Slab City. That was in World War II, when the area was a Marine training base. After the war, the base was shut down and the government took out the buildings.

But it left behind the concrete slabs they had stood on. Soon vagabonds and snowbirds discovered the huge free campground in the California desert. They called it Slab City because those first arrivals camped on the abandoned slabs.

The government also left behind several storage tanks. These have also become homes to Slabbers, including Louis and Ernetta.

Louis's tank is midway between Salvation Mountain and the Slab City hot springs, because of course America's biggest homeless camp would have its own hot springs and religious shrine.

It's early evening when I pass the abandoned guard shack painted with the Slab City slogan—"The Last Free Place"—and turn down the sandy path that winds through the cactus and mesquite to Louis's tank.

It's circular, maybe forty feet high and sixty across, and made of concrete faded to a pale desert beige. A bank of solar panels is visible along the south slope of the roof.

Murals adorn the outside of the tank. One of them features rattlesnakes writhing up out of the desert sand, right above a cute little redheaded cartoon girl with huge eyes.

Another features two pensive blue women with manicured nails and gorgeous hair that morphs into feathers as it drapes down their backs. One rides through the ocean depths astride a huge blue whale, the other a giant squid.

Louis lives in a tank because of his sensitivity to electromagnet emissions. He believes the steel rebar in the concrete walls create a Faraday cage, guaranteed to exclude such emissions. He can stand them long enough to do his job at the sheriff's office, he says, but he needs eight hours a day in the tank to recover.

Ernetta doesn't work—or can't, I'm not sure which—but she can and does take care of Louis, including never letting his food touch, so that's their partnership. He's the wage-earner, she's the caregiver.

When I pull up to their tank, the temperature is down to a bearable 88 degrees as the sun slides toward the Santa Rosa Mountains west of the Salton.

Ernetta stands at the end of a picnic table under a palo verde tree in full spring bloom with big yellow flowers. She's smoking a cigarette and grilling something on a hibachi. Nearby, along the tank wall, is Louis's chicken coop of scrap two-by-fours and wire mesh with an old parachute draped over the top for shade.

There's no sign of Louis, so I assume he's still asleep. The tank door is closed, and bears a hand-painted sign: "Welcome to Camp Faraday—Keep Away from My Chickens!"

Ernetta is fiftyish, stringy gray hair, shorts, t-shirt, no bra, flip-flops, and skinny. I suspect that's from a fondness for meth, the drug of choice in the Slabs. But she does have all of her teeth except for one canine on the bottom left, so maybe not. On the other hand, Louis makes a decent salary at the sheriff's office, and there's no rent or utilities in Slab City, so where does the money go? I don't judge, or ask questions.

"Dana," she says as I step out of the Jeep. "You bring the shakes?"

"Absolutely." I open the rear hatch, haul the cooler over to the picnic table and show her the three calorie bombs on ice.

"That's good," she says. "You tend to my snake here and I'll get Louis up. Don't let it burn, now."

She hands me the barbecue fork, and goes into the tank. I take a closer look at what's on the hibachi. Sizzling over the charcoal is a big coil of meat as thick as my forearm. It can only be rattlesnake, another downside of life in the Slabs in addition to meth, poverty, mental illness, and chicken thieves.

I keep the snake moving with the barbecue fork so it doesn't scorch, as Louis's hens peck and cluck in their coop.

After a few minutes, Louis and Ernetta emerge. Louis is round-faced with wide-set hazel eyes and bowl-cut brown hair thinning on top now. He has a fluffy build and a big uncertain smile, as if he's never sure what expression is appropriate to the situation. I want to hug him, but he doesn't like that.

He lifts a shake from the cooler, takes a bench at the table, and draws a big loud slurp with no thanks, hello or eye contact. That's Louis.

"Hi," I tell him. He still doesn't make eye contact, but he does say "Hello, Dana."

Ernetta relieves me at the hibachi and gives the snake a flip.

I hand her a shake, get one for myself, and ask her about the snake.

"Diamondback," she says. "Nice one, huh?"

I nod and put on an impressed look.

"He got into my chickens, Dana," Louis says.

"Last time he'll do that," Ernetta says. "Live and let live is all well and good but we won't tolerate an egg thief. And diamondback is mighty tasty."

I check Louis's progress. He's about halfway through the shake.

"Anything new out here?" I ask.

Ernetta gives me a quick rundown as we work on our shakes.

A Slabber named Woolly Bear drowned in the hot springs a couple weeks back, but it looks to have been a seizure, not drugs or foul play.

A convicted child molester named Rando Dando had his camp burned down and left the Slabs. Fire is the traditional way of ridding the Slabs of undesirables, especially child molesters.

And an entire camp of Slabbers has gone missing, with nobody knowing for sure where to. Two women named Moxie and Sunflower, Sunflower's baby boy Can-Am, a cat named Whiskers, and a guy named Bro-Man.

"I heard Sunflower might be in jail for attempted murder," Ernetta says. "And Moxie might have a broken finger. And Bro-Man might be in the hospital with a bullet in his stomach. And they're saying another camp took Whiskers and CPS took Can-Am."

"It's always something out here, right?"

"Especially with that Sunflower," Ernetta says. "She needs to swear off men."

"Who doesn't?" I say. We share a just-us-girls laugh.

Louis finishes his shake with a last long slurp, belches, and returns the cup to the cooler. Trash disposal is another of the many unsolved challenges of life in the Slabs, so I don't mind hauling his empty back to civilization.

"488 days, Dana," he says, still without eye contact.

That's another thing about Louis. He never forgets a date, and he can tell how many days are between any two dates without thinking about it.

"I don't count how long it is since Frank got shot, Louis. But that sounds right."

"It is correct," he says. "Do you continue to experience sadness, Dana?"

"Yes, I still grieve sometimes."

This kind of thing is like a catechism with Louis, something to be endured to get to what I'm here for.

"The maximum temperature in Palm Springs was 59 that day," he goes on. "The president was meeting with an African delegation at the White House. But the vice president was not present. Do you need his address or phone number, Dana?"

"No thanks, Louis. But I do need your help with something else."

"Please explain, Dana."

I say I need to track a vehicle from Caliente Springs through the traffic camera system to see if it was near a certain address in Palm Springs on a certain day, but it has to be a secret. He can't tell anybody except Ernetta.

"That will not be difficult, Dana," he says.

"You cool with this?" I ask Ernetta.

"It's not gonna get him in trouble at work?" She lifts the snake off the grill, drops it onto a platter, and starts cutting it up with her belt knife.

"Not if they can't find out he was in the ALPR system."

"They cannot find that out, Dana," Louis says.

Ernetta nods and says, "Okay. Ever eat diamondback, Dana?"

"Can't say I have."

"Tastes just like rabbit," she says. "Want some?"

"Sure," I say. "Why not?"

She disappears into the tank.

I show Louis the photo I took of the license plate on Efren Mendoza's car outside the house where the Chaplain and I found him dead. And I give him the address of Barney's compound in Mira Las Palmas.

"What I need to know," I say, "is if that car was anywhere near that address on the morning of April 15."

"Why do you require this information, Dana?"

"Something bad happened there that day, and Efren Mendoza may have been involved."

"I will obtain the ALPR information for you, Dana."

He goes into the Faraday tank, returns with a Lenovo laptop, sets it on the picnic table, and plugs it into a power outlet at the bottom of an electrical conduit running down the tank wall from his roof-top solar array. Ernetta follows him out with plasticware, paper plates, an open can of baked beans, and three bottles of water. Pretty soon we've all got servings of snake and beans in front of us.

Louis bends over to inspect his. "Don't worry," Ernetta says. "They're not touching."

"Thank you, Ernetta," Louis says. "Dana is your food adequately separated?"

"It is," I say. "And thank you, Ernetta."

On her plate, I see, the beans are heaped piled on top of the rattlesnake meat. She looks at Louis as if daring him to say something.

He doesn't. Instead, he cranks up the laptop and connects it to Ernetta's cell phone via a USB cable.

"We got no wi-fi out here," she says. "Somehow he gets the Internet off my phone."

I move behind Louis to watch him work.

He shuts the laptop. "You are not allowed to see this," he says. "You are no longer employed by the Coachella County Sherriff's Office, Dana. I will brief you on what I find."

As Louis works and eats his dinner, I try a bite of rattlesnake and chew with caution. It's not bad, but neither does it make me want diamondback ever again. Or rabbit. I do finish it, though, out of politeness and hunger.

"That was delicious," I tell Ernetta. "My compliments to the chef."

"Thanks," she says. "Take some home?"

"Absolutely," I say. I don't bother to tell her I'm sure Duke will love it. In fact, he once caught a rattler behind the house and ate everything but the head and rattles, which I discovered on the patio the next morning. It was his idea of a gift, I think.

Finally Louis closes the laptop, hands Ernetta her phone, and says "Miss Ernetta, you must go inside now. As a non-LEO, you are not allowed to hear what Dana and I will discuss."

Ernetta says, "Of course, Louis," and takes her plate of rattlesnake into the tank.

"Dana, the outcome is negative," Louis says.

"Negative?"

"The vehicle was not present in Palm Springs on the specified day. It appears to have stayed within Caliente Springs since it left Riviera Dunes on the twelfth of April, Dana."

"Are you sure? It's really imp—"

The hair rises on the back of my neck as it sinks in.

"It was in Riviera Dunes? On April 12? What time of day was this?"

"At precisely 7:07pm on April 11, one day earlier, the monitoring system recorded the vehicle's entry onto Interstate 10 at the Gene Autry Trail junction presumably after its departure from Caliente Springs. Subsequently at 7:17 p.m., the vehicle was recorded exiting Interstate 10 onto Route 86 in the vicinity of Indio. The vehicle's next recorded appearance was at 7:49pm by the Riviera Dunes ALPR. It is inferred that the vehicle exited the highway at this juncture, as there were no further ALPR detections until it was recorded again by the Rivera Dunes ALPR at 7:59 a.m. on April 12, this time proceeding in a northbound direction as it was recorded re-entering the Interstate from Route 86 at Indio at 8:31 a.m. and was recorded exiting at the Gene Autry Trail at 8:46 am, which suggests a return to Caliente Springs, Dana."

This comes out so fast and flat in Louis's monotone that it takes me a while to process.

"So this vehicle was in Riviera Dunes from the night of April 11 until just before eight o'clock on April 12?" I ask. "Is that right?"

"Correct," Louis says. "Until 7:59 a.m., Dana."

Which means Efren Mendoza was there around the time Jamie Lochner showed up and supposedly found the body of Tony Alvarez.

"Are you sure?" I ask Louis.

"Yes," Louis says. "Did you want to know about the preliminary autopsy report as well, Dana?"

It takes a few seconds, then I realize what he must be talking about. "On Efren Mendoza? Sure, Louis."

"He was killed by a single round from a .45."

"No surprise there," I say. "I saw the body and it had a pretty big hole in the chest. Anything else on that case in the files?"

"Nothing," he says. "People in the office are saying the investigators are stuck. Mr. Mendoza was allegedly a small-time drug dealer and they think he was killed by a customer. Or by a supplier. And they are not very interested, Dana."

"Sounds like the cops we all know and love, Louis," I say. "Am I right?"

"You are correct up to a point, Dana. But you were not like that as I recall, Dana."

"I'm still not like that, Louis."

"Do you wish any other information regarding the parties in this case? The preliminary autopsy reports are available on Mr. Alvarez and Mr. Lochner as well, Dana."

"Any surprises there?"

"None that I am aware of. The reports confirm that both also died by gunshot, as stated in the news, Dana. I will notify you know if there are any updates in the various cases."

"Thank you, Louis."

Chapter Seventeen

I PULL OUT OF THE SLABS and head north as the sun drowns itself in the Salton Sea. I call Ike and brief him on what I've learned, and we agree to meet the next morning.

I spend the rest of the trip wishing they had phones for dogs so I could let Duke know I'm on my way home with a ziplock of grilled rattlesnake for him. That, and fighting a nagging feeling that I'm missing something about the .45 that killed Efren Mendoza.

When Ike and I convene for breakfast in a back booth at Sheldon's Deli the next morning, he's still processing the news.

"Our dead hitman killed Tony Alvarez?" he says. "Seriously?"

A waitress with "Elena" on her nametag comes up to take our order. I put my response on hold while we tell her we want two black coffees and two schmears—lox and cream cheese on poppy seed bagels.

"*Bueno*," she says, and bustles away.

Sheldon's is another Palm Springs institution that should not exist in the middle of the California desert, yet there it is. A traditional New York-style Jewish deli, except the staff is mostly Latino and the menu features baby back ribs across from the borscht and bagels. Go figure.

"So," Ike picks up the thread. "Our dead hitman killed the guy who hired him?"

"To all appearances. People lie, but ALPRs don't."

"So Jamie didn't do it, then?"

"No way, I'm thinking."

"But you say they were in Rivera Dunes at the same time that morning. Maybe she hands him the gun, he kills Tony with it, she pays him and takes it back, then she kills Barney with it three days later."

Elena arrives with our schmears, sets them down, and says "Enjoy!"

I take a long sip of coffee while I work out how to make my case to Ike. Finally I decide there's nothing for it but to dive in. "I think Jamie's been telling us the truth all along. She didn't do it. Any of it."

"Come on. Without her, how do you explain Tony being killed with her gun, and Barney too?"

"Nielle."

"What?"

"Nielle. She was behind all of it. Tony, Barney, the hitman, all of it."

"How do you know that?"

"Look yonder."

I point to the waiting area just inside the entrance and wave Jamie Lochner over.

"Something tells me I've been set up," Ike says as she slides into the booth beside me.

"Did you tell him?" she asks.

"Nope. Better he should hear it from you."

"Hear what?" Ike says.

"Remember when Ray Jefferson from the Brawley sheriff's station interviewed Jamie about Tony's murder?" I ask. "She said—"

"Remember it! First time I ever had a client's husband get murdered while she was being questioned for killing her lover."

"Sure. But do you remember Jamie telling Jefferson about the trip to Joshua Tree for target practice with Barney?"

"When they shot up the abandoned cars?"

"Right. And do you remember what she said about their guns?"

Ike shrugs.

"Jamie, what did you tell me when I called you at two o'clock this morning and asked what kind of gun Barney had?"

"I said I didn't know, but it was way louder and bigger than mine and he called it the Terminator. Just like I told the police."

"Why does that name ring a bell?" Ike asks

I bring up the *Terminator* Wikipedia page on my phone and scroll down to the photo of Arnold Schwarzenegger holding his .45 Hardballer Longslide. "And is this the gun?"

I hand Jamie the phone.

"Yeah, that looks like Barney's gun."

"Pass Ike the phone."

She does.

He studies it for a few seconds. "So Barney Lochner had a .45. So what?"

"Yeah," Jamie says. "So what?"

"Efren Mendoza was killed with a .45."

The resulting silence stretches on and on, then Ike breaks it. "And this was what, six days after Barney was killed with Jamie's gun?" He looks at Jamie. "By which time, as noted, you were in cold storage at the Parsons. Which leaves—"

"It leaves Nielle," I say. "If the Terminator killed Efren Mendoza, Nielle did it. There's no other realistic possibility. And that has to mean she somehow did the rest of it, too, with Mendoza's help. And therefore, Jamie's innocent."

"Told you!" Jamie says.

"Do we know if a .45 was found on the Lochner property after Barney's murder?" Ike says.

"We do. I contacted the Chaplain after I spoke with Jamie, and he checked with his contact at Palm Springs Public Safety to see if they found any firearms on the property other than Jamie's Ruger."

"And?"

"And the crime scene techs did find a .45 Hardballer during the search after Barney's death."

"And are you going to tell us where they found it?"

"In Nielle's pool house. She told them, and I quote, 'Daddy gave it to me.'"

"I remember that now!" Jamie says. "It was after the Joshua Tree trip. Barney gave her the Terminator because of the same home invasion as why he gave me the Ruger."

"Exactly what Nielle told the investigators."

"Well, I'll be damned, Ike says.

"Indeed," I say. "Nielle hired a hitman to kill Tony and Barney under circumstances that would make it look like Jamie did it, then she killed the hitman."

Another silence as Ike thinks it over. "How would she contrive to put Mendoza and Jamie at the scene of Tony's murder at the same time?"

"Nielle knew Jamie had hired me," I say. "So it was an easy guess I was supposed to find Tony for her. Nielle had a tracker on my Jeep, so she knew I went to Riviera Dunes and spent some time at Manny's the morning after Jamie hired me. Another easy guess was that I had found Tony there, and that Jamie would be going down herself to see him. So, she stole Jamie's .22 from her Mercedes, gave it to Mendoza, and sent him down to Riviera Dunes to wait. Nielle also had a tracker on Jamie's Mercedes, so when she started down to Manny's that morning, Nielle knew right away. She gave Mendoza Jamie's arrival time, and the rest is history."

"That is definitely something Skeeter would do," Jamie says. "The bitch."

"It's pretty complicated," Ike says. "But I guess it could work."

"What did Nielle have to lose?" I ask. "If Jamie doesn't show up, she sends Mendoza back to Caliente Springs and they wait for another opportunity. Or maybe his orders are to kill Tony regardless, but he gets paid double if he makes it look like Jamie did it."

"At which he succeeded admirably," Ike says. "But tell me more about the .45 piece of this. How do we even know Mendoza was killed with one?"

"Let's just say somebody told me what's in the preliminary autopsy report."

"Would this be the same somebody who told you about Mendoza and the ALPRs?"

"Exactly. And he says the sheriff's office is stuck on the case, and not too interested. No suspects, no leads, no murder weapon, just a small-time drug dealer with a .45 size-hole in his chest. Sometimes known as a why-bother."

"And how interested are the Palm Springs investigators in Nielle's good friend the Terminator?"

"Not at all interested. It's irrelevant to their case, since Barney was killed with Jamie's Ruger 22."

"So they haven't connected Nielle to Mendoza's death?"

"Nope. Caliente Springs, where Mendoza was killed, is under the jurisdiction of the county sheriff's office."

"And Palm Springs hasn't told the sheriff's office about finding a .45?"

"No reason to think so, no."

"These agencies don't talk to each other?"

"You'd be surprised how much they don't."

"Let's review," Ike says. "Neither agency, not the sheriff's office nor Palm Springs Public Safety, is aware that the Mendoza and Lochner murders may be connected."

"That seems to be the case. We're the only ones who know."

"Is there any actual evidence linking Nielle to Mendoza?" Ike asks.

"Not that we know of," I say.

"Do we know if the Terminator is still on the property?"

"We don't, sorry."

"Could the Chaplain find out for us?"

"I asked him about that. He says his contact at Palm Springs Public Safety got pretty interested in why he wanted to know about the Lochner search, so we need to let that line go quiet for a while or we may tip our hand."

"Regrettable," Ike says. "If Nielle used it to kill Mendoza, she has likely disposed of it, so if it's missing, that would be significant."

"Agree. So what now?"

"Obviously we tell the police everything," Jamie says. "We just solved their whole case. They arrest Skeeter for killing everybody and they drop the charges against me and I live happily ever after."

Ike and I exchange a raise of the eyebrows.

"Right?" Jamie says.

"Not exactly," he says.

"Not hardly," I say.

"Why not?" Jamie asks.

"If Nielle didn't do it or if she did but the police can't find the Terminator," Ike says, "all we'd do is alert them to Mendoza's involvement in the case. They follow the same line of investigation as Dana did and discover that you and Mendoza were in Riviera Dunes at the same time the morning Tony was killed. They add a count of conspiracy to commit murder to the charges against you and we're worse off than before."

Ike pauses and looks at Jamie. "But it would tie up a lot of loose ends."

"You still think I did it!" Jamie says.

"What I think is that I have to remain open to all possibilities," Ike says. "Either way, you'll get a vigorous defense."

"Dana," Jamie says, "you know I'm innocent, right?"

"Let's just say it's my working assumption."

"But wait," Jamie says. "What if they do prove the Terminator killed Mr. Mendoza? Then I'm in the clear, right?"

"Probably," Ike says. "Eventually. Ballistics is not an exact science, but if they do get a match, so many dots will start to connect up that the police won't be able to dismiss it as mere coincidence, no matter how they much want to hang it all on you. They'll know Nielle had to be involved because of the apparent match on the .45 rounds from Efren's body and the backstop."

"But they still won't know how it all fits together," I say to Jamie. "Like, why was Efren in Rivera Dunes the same time as you when Tony was killed? And why would Nielle hire a hitman to kill both her father and your lover? So, they would—"

"It's what I said before," Jamie says. "She had Tony killed to break my heart, and she had her father killed because he broke her heart by loving me more than her. And she framed me for both of them so I'd spend the rest of my life in jail."

"Maybe so, maybe no," Ike says. "But what matters is, they keep digging, this thing drags on forever, and who knows what they'll come up with? Maybe it helps us in the end, but, short term, there's just too many uncertainties to risk it."

"To risk what?"

"Telling the police what we know," I say. "First we have to find out if Nielle was linked to Efren Mendoza."

Chapter Eighteen

I'M STARTING THE JEEP in the Sheldon's parking lot when Lita's face comes up on my phone.

"Dana," she says. "Can you come down to Mom's?"

"Right now? What's up?"

A couple of seconds pass in silence.

"Lita? What's going on?"

"Mom is going back to Hermosillo."

"What? Why?"

"It's the immigration raids. Her cousin down in Calexico got caught outside a Home Depot and now she's freaking out. She's afraid they'll get her, too. So she's going back till things cool off up here, if they ever do."

"Maybe Ike can—"

"No, she got deported once before. She says she'll go to jail if they catch her again."

"Hermosillo? How far is that?"

"I don't know," Lita says. "Far. The flight is over five hours and Mom has to change planes twice."

"Is she taking Sonny and Rose?"

"That's why she wants to talk to you."

Fifteen minutes later, I pull into the driveway at Yolanda's two-story bungalow in Chapel City southeast of Palm Springs. Faces are browner here, and real estate is cheaper.

The place is neat and clean with white stucco walls, blue trim, and a tile roof. A bright red front door, set back into the shade of a stucco arch, is bordered by ceramic planters overflowing with green dwarf palms. Vertical white shades dress the front windows.

Lita has the door open before I'm out of the Jeep.

"Dana, Dana," she says. "Come in, come in."

I do, and she leads me to the kitchen doorway. Yolanda's at the big wooden dining table with a phone to her ear.

"My god!" she says. "That's the earliest you can get me there?"

She's silent for a few seconds, then, "*Bueno*, if that's all you have right now."

She scribbles notes on the back of an envelope, then taps off the call and wipes her eyes on a napkin.

Through an open door behind her, I see two big wheelie suitcases open on a double bed. They're half full of clothes and surrounded by more clothes, piles of toiletries, a bible, a framed picture of the twins, and a hair dryer.

"Dana," she says. "Lita told you?"

"I am so sorry to hear it."

She sniffles and dabs her eyes with a napkin. "*Siempre pasa algo.*"

"'It's always something,'" Lita whispers.

"I know that," I whisper back.

"Dana, you have a seat," Lita tells me. "I'll make tea."

She busies herself at the stove as I take a chair across from Yolanda.

Yolanda is plump, with threads of silver winding through a loose, fat braid that drops over one shoulder. She has kind brown eyes like her daughter's. Today she also has a stressed but determined mouth.

"So, ah, Lita says we need to talk about Sonny and Rose, but if this isn't a good time, I could—"

"No, no," she says, "it must be now."

"Okay, what do—"

"Oh, Dana," she says, "you know how much I love the twins and I want to take them with me, but I don't know if I can ever come back. And what would I do with them down there? I don't even know if I can take them out of this country before the adoption is final."

Lita brings in steaming mugs of tea and sets them before us. I put in honey and lemon to stall for time.

"We can probably make it work for a while without Mom," she says. "Dad's gone a lot with his trucking job, but I'm here except for my paralegal classes and when you need me. But Sylvia and I are getting married in the fall and I'm going to Stanford. So if Mom's not back by then..."

"They might have to go into foster care." Yolanda stirs her tea and looks at me.

"Foster care?"

"*Sí, w*hen I was getting Sonny and Rose, the adoption agency told me there are many nice foster families out there."

"I hear it's the luck of the draw, though," Lita says.

"*Sí.*" Yolanda nods. "The luck of the draw."

I study my tea to avoid contact with the two pairs of big guileless eyes gazing at me.

"I'd love to take them," I say. "But..."

"But what?" Lita says.

"But, you know, I've never dealt with kids, not full time, and I'm gone a lot with my work, and my place is way up in the hills with almost no neighbors and a lot of coyotes and rattlesnakes."

Yolanda nods. "*Los niñitos* will be if they are just in a place with people who love them. You love them and they love you, Dana. You're their *tia*."

"I know," Lita says. "You could move down here. They're used to this place and it's close to Brighter Day."

"What? Where?"

"Here. You and Duke could move down here and stay in Mom's house while she's in Mexico. That way the twins would still feel at home."

Yolanda stares at her daughter. "What about your father? I don't know—"

"We have the spare bedroom," Lita says. "And Dad will probably come see you a lot in Hermosillo a lot anyway, right?"

Yolanda nods with a thoughtful expression. "*Sí, es posible.*"

"Will Gabriel be okay with this?" I ask.

"He will if I say so."

"Smart husband. Is he safe from the raids? And you, Lita?"

"I think so. He's a naturalized citizen, and I was born here."

Once again the four eyes focus on me like laser beams. "Please, Dana," Yolanda says.

"Why do I feel surrounded?"

Lita glances at the wall clock behind Yolanda, and says, "Look at the time! We have to get them ready for Brighter Day."

She opens a bedroom door and yells, "Hey, guys, time for *Dinosaur Train*! And *Tia* Dana is here!"

As Rose and Sonny toddle out, she hands me the remote. "You start it for them while I get breakfast together, okay?"

I find *Dinosaur Train* on the living room TV, build a pile of cushions in front of it, and we snuggle in to watch a baby T-Rex named Buddy and his family take an undersea train to meet Carla, a baby shark with long dark eyelashes.

"Get eyelashes like Carla," Rose says.

"Drive Buddy's train!" Sonny says.

A few more moments of bliss, then Lita calls us to breakfast at the dining table. We dig into Cheerios with milk and bananas.

Halfway through, Lita speaks up with a sideways glance at me.

"Hey, guys, Mom is going to Mexico for a while. How would you like it if *Tia* Dana stays with us while she's gone?"

Rose talks over the top of her orange juice cup. "Sleep with me, *tia*?"

"Dukie come, too?" Sonny chimes in.

I shoot Lita a look. "I have to think about this."

I'm halfway home when I hear his voice from the back seat. "I don't want them leaving the country. Or in foster care."

I catch the smell of Partagas smoke as I adjust the rear view mirror. And there he is, Imaginary Frank, Stetson in place, arms spread along the top of the backrest, cigar between the first two fingers of his right hand, cocksure as ever.

"I thought you'd feel that way," I tell him.

"You know everything I know."

"Yep, I do."

"If you'll lower a window I'll let the smoke out," he says.

"I don't mind. Anyway, it's imaginary. Like you."

"Then why am I here?"

"You tell me."

"To help you figure out how you feel about sending my twins to Mexico?"

"Good guess."

"So, what about it? You couldn't come up with either 'Hell, no' or 'God, yes' back there."

"I'm stuck," I say. "They're all I've got left of you, but I'm no mother and I work all the time. And they should have an adult male in their lives."

"Right." He draws on the Partagas in silence.

"My life would be simpler if you could have kept your zipper up, you know."

"Jennifer bowled me over the second I saw her. Just like you did."

"Bullshit."

"It's honest bullshit, though."

I have to chuckle. "Dead or alive, same old Frank."

"At your service. So?"

"So what do I do?"

"You're right about one thing. It would be nice if they had an adult male in their life."

"I know. I was raised without a father and I wouldn't wish that on any kid."

"I know how you hurt. But maybe he could come in from the shadows."

"What? Who could?"

Too late, he's gone. No a goodbye, just like the night he was killed. I lower the rear windows to let out the imaginary Partagas smoke, then I bring up Cinder on my phone.

Chapter Nineteen

AFTERGLOW is like everything else in sex. Different men deal with it in different ways.

One cop I dated would finish, roll over, let me rest my head on his chest for a bit, then get up and dress. He would say one word—"Goodbye"—and take off like my bed was a crime scene.

He didn't last long.

Frank would also let me rest my head on his chest, but he'd fall asleep instead of leaving. I liked that, the light snore, the rise and fall of his breathing, the CHECK-me, CHECK-me, CHECK-me of his heartbeat. Most people claim to hear LUB-dub, LUB-dub, LUB-dub. I don't. I've never been able to hear anything but CHECK-me, CHECK-me, CHECK-me.

The Chaplain doesn't make a fast getaway, nor does he fall asleep. He lies there with my head on his chest, smokes a Partagas, drinks Jack and Diet Coke, and tells stories of his adventures with the Moguls.

Disaster stories, of course. I've never met a man who tells stories with happy endings. Funny sometimes, but never happy.

Just now he's finishing a story about a run to Yuma.

The point of the story, it turns out, is not what the Moguls did in Yuma, nor is it why they went. It's that the Chaplain never made it because he hit a coyote near the exit to a desert hamlet called Felicity.

"I should have been paying attention. Next thing the coyote is under me, I lose the bike, and I slide down the Interstate on my butt feeling glad I wore leathers this time."

"Because I nagged you into it, if you'll remember."

"Respect, *cariño.*" He kisses my forehead. "So one of the brothers gave me a ride into Felicity. I rented a flatbed to bring the bike back up here. Now I have to rebuild it. That's why I'm on the Indian tonight."

"I was wondering about that," I lie. All motorcycles a real biker would be caught dead on look the same to me, which is why I didn't notice he wasn't on his Harley when he pulled onto my patio about twenty minutes ago.

Yes, twenty. Because that's all it takes with us, the first time. Then there's a recovery period and the next round is slower and even nicer.

It's the recovery period we're in now, and he's talkative. They say the quickest way to a man's heart is through his stomach, but I find the zipper is pretty quick, too. I figure it's time to dive in.

"Yolanda may take Frank's twins to Hermosillo."

He rolls out from under me and sits up. "*¿Que?*"

"She's freaking out about the immigration raids so she's going back home for a while, maybe for good. She may take Sonny and Rose with her. Or she might put them in foster care."

"Frank wouldn't like either one."

"That's what he said."

"Imaginary Frank showed up again?"

"He did," I say.

"Huh."

"Yolanda wants me to take them so they can stay here in Palm Springs. I'm moving into her place while she's gone. I'm down there all the time anyway."

"I guess it makes sense. Will we still…"

"Of course. But I don't want to raise them without a man in their life. I know what that's like. I grew up without a father."

"Same," he says. "It's why I ended up in jail."

"They do need a father figure since theirs got himself killed."

"*Verdad.*"

"Frank thinks you should come in from the shadows and be that figure. So do I."

"But I'm a felon."

"I talked to Ike and he thinks it's doable. It's been over ten years since the meth bust and it was under five grams and your record is clean since then. And at the time you were a heroin addict dealing meth to feed your habit. But you went through rehab and now you're a confidential police informant."

"Which could get me killed if it came out."

I let him work on it in his own way. I'm not an expert on men, but I know one thing. When they need their space you have to give it to them.

"Come in from the shadows," he says at last. "And do what?"

"You could work with me. We'd be Forsythe and Associates."

He draws on the Partagas and chuckles. "An associate. Me."

"Yep."

Another silence, then, "I think about it sometimes, not living in the dark. It's cold and lonely, mostly. Not so much since we got together, but still most of the time. I just couldn't think of a way."

"Maybe this is it."

"Uh-huh." Another long silence, then, "If I don't step up, could this be the end of us?"

"I don't want you gone from my life. But down at some level I didn't know I had, there's a voice saying, 'a real man steps up.' Is that old-fashioned?"

"Maybe it's hard-wired, *cariño*. I hear it, too." He draws on the cigar. "If you eventually adopted Rose and Sonny, they would have a mother in a risky profession. Like their father."

"I can handle it. I was a cop who didn't get shot, you know. Unlike Frank, I don't trust anybody. And you'd be with me, right?

"Always."

"Like now, except with daylight."

He chuckles. "I'd have to leave the Moguls."

"Can you do that?"

"If they don't think you're gonna cause trouble. You can even keep your colors. But I could never work on anything involving them."

"Is that a yes, then?"

"It's a maybe," he says. "I have to think about it."

"I'll set up a meeting with Ike."

"Enough business." He stubs out the Partagas in the bourbon glass, and covers my mouth with his.

Quite some time later, he's lighting another Partagas as he pads toward the kitchen with his bourbon glass.

"No more of that," I yell after him. "We have work to do."

"What? Where?"

"The Rattlesnake."

Chapter Twenty

HE CLAMPS A PARTAGAS between his teeth, straddles the Indian and kicks it to life. I climb on behind and wrap my arms around him. We dive through the night toward the lights of Palm Springs. As usual, I'm wearing a helmet and he's not. At least he's got the headlight on. The moon has set while we were busy inside, so the drive down from the Cahuilla foothills is dark as only the desert night can be.

Forty minutes later, he shuts off his chrome horse in front of the Rattlesnake.

It's not much to look at. Single story, gray cinder block, neon "Rattlesnake" sign on the roof with a coiled diamondback, fangs-bared, between "RATTLE" and "SNAKE." The 'K' in snake is trying to burn out, so the sign winks at us.

"You go in and scope it out, *sí?*" the Chaplain says.

I hand him my helmet and slip inside.

My job is to make sure the place is free of cops and Moguls. I pause to let my eyes adjust. In the corner, a couple playing shuffleboard, At the bar, two men drinking Coronas and arguing in Spanish about *futbol*, behind the bar a woman with hair the color of dried blood dangling a live white mouse over an aquarium.

I crack open the door, lean out and give the Chaplain a thumbs-up, then walk to the bar for a closer look at the redhead. She gives me a fast glance, raises the lid, and drops the mouse into the aquarium. The diamondback coiled in a corner lifts its head, contemplates the mouse for thirty seconds, then lowers its head again. As if to say, "All the time in the world, little buddy."

The mouse doesn't move. Except for the pink nose, which twitches.

The barmaid points at the aquarium. "That's Cascabel," she says. "Our mascot. What can I get you?"

I want a Moscow Mule, but my inner voice tells me the Rattlesnake is no place to order a girly drink. I order two Jacks and Diet, and study the barmaid while she builds them.

Maybe she was a looker once. Good bones, nice boobs that might be real. But now she's skinny and stringy-haired, rough-skinned, with a cold sore at the right corner of her mouth.

This, I surmise, must be the Chaplain's old girlfriend Cristal, the one who told him where Efren lived.

She's wearing a white pullover with long sleeves. Perhaps that's to cover needle tracks, but right now her vibe is pretty straight. If she's not clean, she must be in that middle phase when a user's no longer high from the last fix but isn't yet Jonesing for the next one.

In a couple minutes she sets the drinks on the bar, along with two napkins and a dish of salted peanuts. "My old boyfriend drank Jack and Diet."

I smile. "Mine still does."

The Chaplain steps in. The shuffleboard players and Corona drinkers fall silent and stare. He stares back, they look away, and the noise resumes.

He spots me at the bar, lets the door bang shut, and comes over. "Cristal," he says as he straddles a stool beside me.

She looks from him to me and back again. "Is this your bitch now?"

"You don't want to be that way," he says. "Not tonight. We need to talk. Come with me."

He leads her to a table in the darkest corner of the Rattlesnake. I follow with the peanuts and drinks and slide into a chair next to him. Cristal is still standing.

"Sit," he says.

She does.

I take out my phone and bring up the photo gallery. At the top are three images I set up before we left the house. One is Nielle Lochner in her brown glasses. The other two are Lita for filler, and Jamie. I push the phone over to Cristal.

"Have you seen any of these women in here?" the Chaplain says.

She glances at the phone. "*No se,*" she says.

I dig a twenty out of my bag and push it over to the Chaplain. He covers it with his hand, the big fingers splayed enough to let Andrew Jackson peer out. Cristal locks eyes with the dead president.

"Now do you remember?" the Chaplain says.

She takes the phone and scrolls up and down through the gallery. Her face says she wants the twenty but maybe not as much as she wants to stay out of whatever trouble the Chaplain has brought into the Rattlesnake tonight.

She shows us the phone and taps Nielle's face. "This one."

I pick up the phone and scroll to Jamie's picture. "Not this one?"

"No, only the one with the big glasses. She took them off when she came in."

The Chaplain glances at me. I nod. He slides the twenty across the table. Cristal disappears it into her bra.

I pass the Chaplain another twenty. He covers it with his hand.

"Who did she talk to?" I ask.

Cristal locks eyes with Andrew Jackson again and tenses up.

"Tell us who it was," I say.

She shakes her head and stares at the wood grain of the table.

"Cristal," the Chaplain says. "Tell us."

"*El moreno.*"

"Efren Mendoza," the Chaplain says. "You're sure?"

"*Verdad.*"

"When was this?" I ask.

Cristal shrugs.

The Chaplain gives her a look and a growl. "How long, Cristal?"

She flinches. "Couple weeks, three maybe."

The Chaplain and I exchange glances. Two weeks would be before Tony's murder, three weeks would be after.

"You can't pin down the exact date?" I ask.

Cristal shakes her head and looks at the Chaplain. "Did you do it?"

"Do what?" I ask. Efren's death hasn't hit the news yet, as far as I know.

"Kill him," Cristal says. "The cops were in here asking around."

"No," the Chaplain says. "He was dead when I found him."

"What did you tell them?" I ask.

"I told them '*No se.*'" Cristal grins in a way that makes me like her a little.

"Bueno," I say with a grin of my own.

She taps the photo of Nielle. "Did this one kill him?"

"What do you think?" the Chaplain asks.

"No se. They sat at this table, Efren's table. They drank beer. They talked. They left. He left a tip."

"Did she give him anything?" he asks.

"A package maybe," Cristal says. "It was dark, I couldn't see."

"Big enough to hold a gun?" I ask.

"Maybe," Cristal says.

The Chaplain pauses for a couple of seconds, bows his head, and looks at her from under his brows until she drops her gaze. "Was she here any other time?"

"Not that I saw. Just one time."

She reaches for the twenty under the Chaplain's fingers. He looks at me and I nod. He moves his hand, Cristal takes the money.

"This woman with the glasses. Will she kill me now for talking to you?"

"She'll never know," the Chaplains says.

"Never," I say.

It's time for Cristal to go back to the bar, but she doesn't. She stays in her chair, eyes on our faces..

"Cristal?" the Chaplain says.

"There was someone else."

"Someone else?" I ask.

"In those pictures." She tilts her head and I sense that she's figured out she can work us. "Someone else met with Efren here."

"Not the white woman I showed you?" I ask.

Cristal shakes her head.

"Who?" the Chaplain asks.

Cristal shrugs. *"No sé."*

The Chaplain frowns, looks at me. I dig out another twenty and slide it over with my phone. The Chaplain covers the bill with his hand.

Cristal shrugs again.

"Jesus Christ," I say. "How much do you want?"

"One hundred," Cristal says.

I look at the Chaplain, who's studying Cristal, who doesn't flinch. He looks at me and nods.

I pass over the four twenties from my bag. The Chaplain stacks them on the first twenty and covers them with his hand.

Cristal picks up the phone, surfs through the gallery, stops at a screen showing the men in the case.

"This one." She pinch-zooms an image and it expands to fill the screen. "He was in here talking with *el moreno.*"

I pull the phone back and stare at the picture of Tony Alvarez.

"Are you sure?"

"*Sí,*" she says. "Tony Alvarez."

"How do you even know his name?"

"He was so cute. I remembered from when I saw his picture on TV after the rich old gringo was killed and they said his name was Tony Alvarez and the blond *gringa* killed him too."

"But you're sure it was him you saw talking to *el moreno*?" I ask.

"I wrote my number on his napkin but he never called."

"And this was when?" the Chaplain asks.

Cristal shrugs. "Maybe a week before the woman with the glasses came in."

He lifts his hand and she disappears the five twenties into her bra. Then she pulls out her phone and starts for the bar.

"Think she's calling her new dealer?" I ask the Chaplain.

"Probably. Cristal may be about to miss a few shifts."

Chapter Twenty-One

...

I WAKE UP in Yolanda's guest room to the sound of small feet padding down the hallway, and try to remember how I got here.

Oh, yeah—after Cristal and the Rattlesnake, I decided I needed some downtime, which means twin time. So I called the ever-gracious Lita from the parking lot and asked if I could slip into the guest room for the night to have breakfast with Rose and Sonny.

The door opens a crack and Rose peers through.

"¿*Tía?* Lita said you were here!"

"That's right, baby. Your *tia* missed you."

She runs to the bed and climbs up with her horsewoman Barbie book. Sonny appears with his Dalmatian book and climbs up, too.

"Read it?" he asks.

I check my phone. 6:47 a.m.

"It's really early, guys. Maybe a nap first?"

"But you're awake," Rose points out with unassailable toddler logic.

They burrow in on either side of me, warm and sleep-rumpled, smelling like Johnson's baby shampoo. I pick up *Fireman Frank* and start reading.

When I finish, Rose looks up. "*Tia*, are you staying forever this time?"

Forever? Jesus.

"Maybe next time," I say.

"Promise?"

"I promise I might."

"Okay, *tia*. Now read Barbie."

As the house comes to life with morning sounds and the smell of huevos rancheros in preparation, I lie there with Frank's orphans curled warm against me and read them *Barbie: Horse Show Champ* and try to decide if this is the life I want.

It's mid-morning by the time Jamie and I rendezvous at Ike's office. Glenn shows us in and brings coffee, I down half a cup at one go. I've had only five hours of sleep since the chat with Cristal.

"Do I even want to know what you and the Chaplain were up to last night?" Ike says with his usual air of martyred patience.

"I do," Jamie says. "How come you wouldn't say on the phone?"

"Nielle Lochner was indeed linked to Efren Mendoza," I say.

"And you know this how?" Ike says.

I give them the short version of our visit to the Rattlesnake.

"Well, I'll be damned," Ike says. "Nielle hired Efren to kill Tony with Jamie's gun?"

"Best guess," I say. "Cristal saw her give him a package the right size."

"Told you," Jamie says. "They had him killed to break my heart. They knew how much I loved him."

"And that's not all," I say.

"Again," Ike says, "do I really want to hear this?"

"You're gonna love it, trust me."

"I doubt that."

"Guess who met with Efren two days before Nielle did?"

Ike pauses for several seconds, eyes closed. I can almost hear the gears grind. Then he sighs. "I can only think of one person. But I don't want to think it. Because it makes even less sense than the rest of this case."

"Who?" Jamie says.

"I think she means Tony," Ike says.

"Aw," Jamie says as she tears up. "He did hire a hitman to kill Barney. He loved me so much."

Ike pinches the bridge of his nose. "Let's review here. We have Tony hiring this hitman, Mendoza, to kill Barney. How come he ended up killing Tony instead?"

"Think about it," I say. "Tony hires him to kill Barney, he scouts Barney's place to figure out how to do it, and he smells big money. He talks to Barney, or maybe Nielle, and he gets a better offer. Next thing you know, it's Tony who's dead."

"That makes as much sense as anything else in this case," Ike says. "You're dumb enough to hire a low-level drug dealer for free-lance hit job, what do you expect?"

"Tony wasn't dumb!" Jamie says. "He was in love!"

"Same difference," Ike says. "But now what? All we have is two meetings in a Latino dive bar. And a heroin addict for a witness."

"What now," I say, "is we need to prove the bullet that killed Efren came from Barney's Terminator .45 via Nielle."

"And without tipping our hand," Ike says. "Because we still aren't sure—"

"Because YOU still aren't sure I didn't do it," Jamie says. "Right?"

"That's only part of it," Ike says. "My rule is, I don't talk to the cops unless I know what I'm talking about, and here I definitely do not."

"It's time for an exception to the rule," I tell Ike. "I want to talk to Ray Jefferson."

"From the county sheriff's office? My God, why?"

"Because Efren's murder is a county case is why." I turn to Jamie. "You said Barney had an indoor firing range in the basement?"

She nods.

"Did he ever go down there and practice with the Terminator?"

"Oh, yeah," she says. "Way more than I ever did with my little Ruger. He and Skeeter both. They loved shooting that thing."

"Is the backstop rubber or metal?"

Jamie closes her eyes in reflection. "Rubber, I think, yeah, black rubber."

"That's a break for us."

"Why's that?"

"Because there's a good chance we can turn up a slug intact enough for ballistics testing. With a metal backstop, forget about it, they get torn to pieces. But rubber? Fifty-fifty at least. We go into the mansion, we dig around in the backstop, and if we find a good slug, we take it to Ray Jefferson and then –"

"That's burglary," Ike says. "We want no part of it. And by we I mean me."

"Can't I authorize it?" Jamie says. "I get half the estate in the will."

"Not if you get convicted of killing Barney," Ike says."

"Which I won't because I didn't!" Jamie says.

"Hopefully," Ike says. "But why not get the Terminator itself?"

"How are we supposed to find it?" I say. "If Nielle killed Efren with it, she probably ditched it. She'd know to do that from all the cop shows she watched with Barney."

Ike sighs. "So you take this hypothetical Terminator round from the backstop to Ray Jefferson and do what?"

"I make him an offer he can't refuse."

I grin.

Ike doesn't.

***

We climb into Jamie's Mercedes convertible and head north up Indian Canyon Drive. As usual, she blasts through the 90-degree heat like she's on a freeway.

"You're gonna get a ticket," I can't stop myself from saying.

She gives me a duck-lipped hot-girl smile and undoes the top button of her sundress. "Not if the cop's male and straight. Or female and gay."

She shoots the first two lights, then catches the one at Arenas Road.

Outside my window, a woman in tennis whites waits for the green with an apricot-colored miniature poodle in rhinestone booties, jeweled leash and matching collar. "That dog's wearing more bling than I own," I say.

Jamie doesn't even glance. "Gloria Mandel. And Jacinto Jack. He gets Botox."

"Seriously."

Jamie nods. "You think it was God made those cute little ears so perky? And he used to pee everywhere, like all these designer dogs, but not anymore. All thanks to Botox."

We pass the art galleries and high-end consignment shops in what our visitors bureau calls the uptown design district. One boutique has nothing in the window but a beige silk scarf draped over a pedestal.

"So," Jamie says as we reach Tachevah Drive and she flicks on the turn signal with a lacquered nail, "You really think we'll find anything usable in the backstop?"

"Fairly good odds, like I said."

Jamie's quiet, eyes on the road, mouth drawn. "He was obsessed with that place. I'd hear him down there shooting at all hours. Said he was working on his groupings."

I glance at her as we swing onto Via La Mira. "What if Nielle's there?"

Jamie taps her Apple watch to life and studies it for a moment. "No worries. She's at her therapist's right now."

"Nielle has a shrink?"

"Oh, yeah," she says. "Lotta raccoons in that attic. She gobbles pills like they were Tic Tacs and trust me, you do not want to see her without them."

Barney's estate rises up on the right with its wrought-iron security fence, the mid-century modern mansion gleaming white and immaculate behind the front gates. The fence is draped with gorgeous purple bougainvillea, except where it's been cleared away for the "ARMED RESPONSE" signs posted at regular intervals.

Jamie swings the Mercedes up to the gates, the security system reads her windshield tag, the gates screech open.

We roll up the curving drive and step out in front of the mansion. It's close to noon now, and already 90 degrees, according to the dash in the Mercedes. Heat boils off the walls and driveway like radiation from a nuclear meltdown.

Jamie leads me down an entry hall that smells of lemon, lavender and never having to ask the price of anything.

The living room opens out like a magazine spread. She sweeps an arm toward the panorama. "Welcome to Chez Lochner."

"Jesus," I mutter. "You could land a Cessna in here."

Jamie half-smiles. "Rich guy's gotta prove it, right?"

She points at a matching pair of low-slung sofas in a luscious cream that's just half a glass of cabernet from catastrophe. "Kagan, Baughman, I can't keep track."

"Never heard of either one," I say.

"Me neither till I married Barney," she says. "It's Skeeter's thing."

Nearby is a group of chairs with spindly metal frames and leather upholstery tufted with leather-covered buttons.

"The chairs I know the name of," she says. "Barcelona. I think."

"I've heard of Barcelona," I say. "I think."

Jamie pauses at a photo wall. Barney holding trophies beside his thoroughbreds, sometimes with Jamie, sometimes without. Barney and Jamie on their wedding day. Barney with Nielle—maybe five or six and clutching Barney's pinkie like she's afraid he'll get away. His smile shows teeth, hers doesn't. It says she'll never be sure that Daddy loves her.

"You know what happens to some of these horses when they can't race anymore?" Jamie asks.

"No idea."

"They get sold for meat and shipped to Canada or Mexico for slaughter. A horse that was worth a million dollars as a two-year-old ends up in a slaughterhouse at six."

"That's dark."

"That's racing. But some of them do get rescued. People retrain them for other work, like pleasure riding or therapy programs. There's even retirement farms for them. I'm going do that kind of thing with our thoroughbred foundation now that Barney's gone. Use his money to help these beautiful animals find second lives." She gives a harsh little laugh. "Assuming I don't end up in jail for the rest of my life, of course."

We reach the arched doorway to the study, still sealed off with crime-scene tape. I deliberate going in anyway, but decide against it. The last thing I need is a charge of evidence tampering.

But I do peer inside. This is where Barney died, however it happened. It's darker than I expect. Not because of bad lighting—the lighting is perfect. Someone cared a lot about how shadows fell in here. You can tell by how the track lights illuminate three oil paintings like saints on an altar. They're all by the same artist, judging by the look and feel of them. Lovers halfway out the door. Men in fedoras who look like they've said too little, too late. A maid and butler holding umbrellas over an elegant young couple dancing in golden sunlight on a misty beach.

Barney's desk sits like a starship command console in the center of the room —wide, polished, and heavy. Rosewood, probably. The kind of thing you buy to let people know you can afford it.

The massive chair that should stand behind the desk is gone, probably taken in for a fine-tooth forensic analysis by Palm Springs Public Safety after his death. A case with rich people getting killed? Cops and prosecutors take no chances. The news people will be breathing down your neck 24-7.

Off to the side, a globe bar stands open like a confessional. Scotch bottles —Macallan, Oban —mostly full, of course. Barney wasn't a drunk, just a guy who never lost control.

Jamie stops at a wall panel next to the study doorway. She swings aside a framed photo—Barney holding a trophy beside another of his thoroughbreds—and taps in a code. The panel hisses sideways to reveal a narrow stairwell with brushed steel walls and caged lighting.

"Barney never let anyone down here but Skeeter and me."

Motion-activated lights buzz to life as we descend and the air gets cooler. At the bottom, Jamie flips a switch and the main lighting snaps on with a low hum.

The room stretches out long and narrow—twenty-five yards easy from firing table to backstop—with walls paneled in black acoustic foam. A motorized target rail runs the length of the ceiling. Human silhouette targets hang from the pulley system. The U.S. military, I seem to recall, found out that a lot of its new boots wouldn't fire at a live human being even in the heat of combat. They switched from the traditional bullseye target to human silhouettes for training the grunts, and problem solved. Maybe Barney heard the same thing.

At the firing line, a custom shooting bench stands bolted to the floor. Dark wood laminated over steel with a non-slip rubber surface, wide enough for weapon rests, ammunition boxes, and ear protection. A padded stool sits beneath it.

Above us, the ventilation system whispers low—a long ductwork spine snaking the ceiling with metal grilles every few yards.

Jamie points. "Barney had it installed special. Hospital-grade filtration. He said he didn't want to breathe lead, just fire it."

Our destination is at the far end: the backstop. A wall of pockmarked black ballistic rubber maybe ten inches thick.

I walk downrange, sweeping the concrete floor with my eyes. It's clean. Either someone vacuumed up the brass or Barney used a shell catcher. Another detail not left to chance.

I run a gloved hand over the surface of the backstop, then fish out my Leatherman and dig into a half-moon tear near the center. A slug emerges, too dented to be usable for ballistics testing, probably from being struck by another incoming round. Same for slugs number two and three. Then comes slug number four, a little dented but whole. I turn it in the light. Definitely a .45, and with clean striations.

I show Jamie. She raises her eyebrows in question.

"Bingo," I say as I drop it into a Ziploc and slide it into my bag.

Chapter Twenty-Two

ON THE WAY BACK to Ike's office, I text Ray Jefferson from the passenger seat of Jamie's Mercedes.

"Need to meet re Efren Mendoza."

He pings back in a few seconds. "Busy, call?"

"Not phone stuff," I answer. "Offline only."

This time it takes a few minutes. Then, "My office, Thermal station, 2 o'clock."

"Works for me," I text.

Jamie drops me in Ike's parking lot. I pick up my Jeep, run by the house to feed Duke and let him out for a pee break, then point the Jeep downhill toward Thermal.

The drive takes nearly an hour in the afternoon heat. Mostly it's south and east along Interstate 10, the big artery that runs through the Coachella Valley like an asphalt carotid. The farther south I go, the browner the hills and the flatter the land. Golf courses give way to wind turbines, irrigation canals, and date palm groves.

I'm about 15 miles out of Thermal when my phone lights up with a call from Ernetta.

"Louis wants to tell you there are some updates," she says.

This rings a bell, but not loud enough that I can remember why. "What updates?" I ask.

"Hang on." Ernetta muffles the phone, probably with her hand, but I can still hear her yell, "Louis! What updates?"

I pick up a distant and indecipherable response from what sounds like Louis's voice, then Ernetta unmuffles. "The cases you were interested in. There are updates."

"Well, what are they?"

More muffled talk, then Ernetta is back. "I'm not allowed to know that because I'm not a former LEO. He'll have to tell you himself."

"Well, then, put him on."

I'm remembering how pointless this suggestion is when Ernetta reminds me. "Dana, you know he won't talk on a phone except the landline at work."

"Oh, right, because of the emissions."

"You'll have to come down here."

"Well, I'm busy," I tell her. "So it'll be a while before I can make it. Unless the update is that maybe Barney Lochner came back to life?"

"You know he doesn't understand jokes, Dana."

"I know, I know," I say. "Just tell him I'll get down there when I can."

What I don't say is that "when I can" is code for "second Tuesday of next week." Why burn a bridge?

Ernetta muffles for a few seconds, then comes back on . "He says don't forget the shakes."

A few minutes later, Thermal comes into sight. It's more of an outpost than a town, with less than 1,500 residents. The sheriff's station sits a block off Airport Boulevard, behind a scrim of low palms and flowering pink and white oleander. Beige stucco building, fading signage, chain-link fencing with concertina wire along the top. It has a resigned, sun-beaten look that says law enforcement facility before you even see the sign.

Several department pickups and one black SUV bake in the parking lot. I pull into a slot marked VISITOR and kill the engine.

Inside, it smells like any aging cop shop—floor wax and old coffee. A receptionist behind bulletproof glass points me to Ray's office, which turns out to be a windowless box with a battered gray desk, two chairs, and a desktop computer that looks like its last software update was during the Obama administration.

Ray is behind the desk in uniform. He's got a notepad open and a thermal mug in front of him that says "Deputy sheriffs can't fix stupid. But we can arrest it."

"So," he says. "What's too hot for the phone?"

I pull the Ziploc out of my bag and set it between us.

Ray bends and squints, but doesn't touch. "Is that a .45?"

I nod. "It is. Complete with an offer you can't refuse."

He rolls his eyes at the old line but he does say, "I'm listening."

"Test this against the round that killed Efren Mendoza. If it's a match, I'll solve the case for you. If not, give it back and I was never here.

He steeples his fingers and cocks his head. "You're working for Ike Skogel on the Jamie Lochner defense, right? So what's a pretty little rich girl like her got to do with a low-level drug dealer getting what they usually get?"

I wait him out. The way I figure it, there's still no reason for him to be aware of the Terminator .45 being found at Barney's mansion since his murder is a Palm Springs case. All Ray is likely to know about .45s is that one was used to kill a drug dealer on his turf.

But he's no dummy. "Maybe I should call my friend Gary Avila and see what he makes of this?" He waves a hand over the Ziploc.

I pick it up and drop it back in my bag. "Not if you ever want to see it again. And, trust me, you do."

"Wouldn't that kind of put you in an awkward situation, sitting on this if it's evidence in a murder case?"

"We don't know that yet, do we?"

He studies me and I can read the math in his eyes. Mendoza's death is a dusty little homicide with no leads, no witnesses, and no heat. Solving it won't make Ray's career, but bungling it might scratch the paint, especially if it's linked to the highly public Jamie Lochner case. What's he got to lose by taking a look inside my Ziploc?

He puts out his hand. "Deal."

"Deal," I say.

We shake and I hand him the Ziploc. "What's your turnaround on ballistics testing lately?"

"Best case, a day or two. It depends."

"On what?"

"On whether my favorite technician's knucklehead kid needs another speeding ticket fixed."

"And you're a guy it's good to know at such times. Nice." I'm halfway out of the chair when I pause for one more shot. "Oh, yeah. Where are you on the Tony Alvarez murder in Riviera Dunes?"

He grins. "Too late, pal. We already shook."

"You can't blame a girl for trying."

"You're extremely trying, Dana. I give you that."

I give him a friendly wave of my middle finger and head out into the blazing heat of a Thermal afternoon.

***

A couple days later, true to his word, Jefferson calls.

"Yes," he says without preamble, "Efren Mendoza was killed by the same .45 that fired your baggie bullet. Now what's this about?"

"Not on the phone," I tell him. "We have to meet. And Avila has to be there."

That afternoon, we gather in Avila's office at Palm Springs Public Safety headquarters. Ray's there, and so is Ike. The office is sleek, modern, and frosted-glass nice, with tasteful desert artwork and just enough chrome to remind you that the taxpayers shelled out a lot of money for it. Coffee, bottled water, and a tray of frou-frou muffins are arrayed on a credenza near the door. I help myself to coffee. Ike grabs a lemon-poppyseed.

Avila sits behind a massive walnut desk with a commanding view of downtown Palm Springs and the Marilyn statue.

Ray, Ike, and I take chairs in front of the desk. Jefferson looks resigned. Avila looks like he already regrets skipping lunch for this. Ike, with his usual doglike hedonism, scatters crumb on his shirt and gobbles the muffin like it's the last one he'll ever eat.

"Okay," Avila says. "Talk."

I lay it out.

Everything.

Starting with Tony Alvarez hiring a hitman to kill Barney Lochner and finishing with me finding the .45 round in Barney's firing range that matches the one that killed Efren Mendoza.

When I finish, Jefferson leans back and blows out a breath. Avila says, "Jesus fuck."

Ike clasps his hands and leans forward.

"Efren Mendoza was killed by Nielle Lochner," he says. "Jamie has a rock-solid alibi for the time of his murder. She was at the Parsons. We're talking security footage, staff witnesses, the security team—she was absolutely there. That leaves only one possibility. Nielle."

"You know we're gonna check with the Parsons," Avila says.

"And you know you're gonna waste your time," I say. "This makes sense only if Nielle hired Efren to kill Tony and then Barney. It had to be Nielle from the start."

Jefferson squints. "But can we really completely rule Jamie out? She still could have killed Tony and Barney, right?"

"Then what were Nielle and Efren doing when they met at the Rattlesnake?" I say. "And why would Nielle kill him with her father's gun?"

"A low-rent drug dealer and a crazy rich girl with daddy issues," Avila says. "Maybe she was a customer."

"Then what was in that package she gave him?" I shoot back. "Because it looked a lot like a gun."

"According to your junkie bartender," Jefferson says.

"Sure," Ike says. "There's still some noise in the data. But this only makes sense if we take Jamie out of the picture. No other explanation even comes close."

They chew on that for a while. Avila starts a sentence with "How about if..." and sputters to a stop. Jefferson says "Or maybe..." and then trails off.

Finally Avila says "Would you excuse us?" He jerks his head at the door and the two cops step out and close it behind them. Through the glass, we can see them in an intense but inaudible discussion. Once Avila points at me and says something. Ray shakes his head and throws up his hands.

More talk, then they nod at each other and come back in.

Jefferson reaches into his shirt pocket and pulls out a Ziploc.

"Here's your baggie," he says with a grin. "But I'm keeping the bullet. It's evidence in a murder investigation now."

"I guess we owe you," Avila says. "You ever want to be a real cop again, give me a call."

"And play by the rules? Been there, done that, no, thanks."

***

A few hours later, I meet Liz Hernandez at the Outrigger, a tiki bar tucked away in a kitschy strip mall in North Palm Springs. It has torches on the walls and servers in lava-lavas who deliver cocktails with tiny umbrellas. The music is surf rock or retro disco, depending on how ironic the manager is feeling. The clientele is 90 percent gay men in everything from muscle tees to caftans, and Liz likes to go there when she needs a break from the male gaze. Which is a serious life issue when you look like Liz—six feet tall, laughing green eyes, and, surname notwithstanding, blonde hair.

Our server tonight is Angelo, a lean, tattooed sweetheart in black nail polish and a silver shark-tooth necklace who calls us "ladies" with such exaggerated reverence you'd think we were royalty. "You're back," he beams. "Let me guess. Hawaiian margarita and a Moscow Mule?"

"Correct," Liz says, and he shows us to our usual corner table.

"You're all aglow tonight," I say in an accusing tone. "Even for you. Something's new."

"His name's Trey," she says. "Works in solar, actually hears what I say and remembers it, and get this—he cooks. Not just grilling dead animals. Real food."

"Next you'll be telling me he flosses."

"Twice a day," she says, and we both laugh. Then she narrows her eyes. "Your turn. How's the mystery biker?

"What can I say. He only comes at night, sometimes he stays over, he has this air of gentle menace."

"And here I am dating a guy who composts," Liz says. "So where's it going?"

"I'm trying to get him to come in from the dark and join Forsythe Investigations. He's got some legal baggage, but I think Ike can straighten it out."

We pause for a moment as Angelo delivers the drinks and says, "Enjoy, ladies."

"You're trying to domesticate him?" Liz picks it up. "You sure you want that?"

"I don't know. Maybe."

"You've always had a weakness for the bad boys," she says "Even Frank had his rough edges, like most cops. Are you really ready for a good boy?"

I think the question over, and decide I don't have an answer.

"Never mind that," I say. "I've got something for you. But you can't use it till it breaks."

She frowns. "Then what's the point?"

"You'll be a hundred miles ahead of the pack, is what."

She chews her lip for a moment. "Okay, but it better be good."

"Trust me. It's huge, better than anything you could make up in a million years."

"You're killin' me here. What is it?"

"There's about to be an arrest in the Barney Lochner and Tony Alvarez murders. And also for that drug dealer killed up in Caliente Springs a few days ago."

Liz is in mid-sip at that moment. She coughs and splutters margarita back into the glass. "Jamie Lochner did all of that?"

"Not Jamie Lochner. Nielle."

"Say what?"

I nod. "Turns out she hired a hitman to kill Jamie's boyfriend, then her own father, and frame Jamie for both murders. Then she killed the hitman to keep him quiet."

"It was definitely Nielle?"

"Yep. The way I put it together, she was jealous of Jamie for stealing her father, and she hated him for loving Jamie."

"Jesus. Talk about a daddy's girl gone bad."

"At least she went big. Just promise me you won't run anything till it happens. I don't want to blow my cover."

"You got it," she says. "But when it breaks, I'm on it like lip gloss on a supermodel. Now walk me through the details."

So I do it all again, just like with Ray Jefferson and Gary Avila. All the way from Tony hiring Efren Mendoza to kill Barney to me finding the Terminator round in Barney's backstop and turning it over to Jefferson.

"Holy shit," she says. "There could be a book deal in this."

"You're welcome," I say.

"From now on, the mules are on me," she says. "Forever."

Chapter Twenty-Three

NIELLE LOCHNER IS ARRESTED three days later for the murders of Barney Lochner, Tony Alvarez, and Efren Mendoza.

The media explode and the story goes national. "Palm Springs Heiress Charged in Triple Homicide" scrolls across the cable news tickers.

Liz's story in the *Desert Herald* digs deepest, complete with timeline, motive, details and sources nobody else has. Her headline reads "Daughter accused of hiring hitman to kill father, mother-in-law's lover."

Liz also does a sidebar on me. I read it standing over the kitchen counter, Duke at my feet, the second half of a bagel cooling beside my coffee mug. I come across as a combination of Supergirl and the Lone Ranger, the plucky lady PI who cracked a case two police departments couldn't crack—or, as Liz hints, wouldn't crack because it involved rich people.

Avila is quoted near the end: "She got lucky. Happens sometimes."

"Thanks for the tip," Liz texts me. "I already got a book feeler from an agent back east."

"Just don't forget the mules," I reply.

My new-found fame sets my phone abuzz, too. A podcaster wants an interview. The booker from a morning cable show asks if I'm free next week. I say "Yes" to the podcaster and "I am" to the booker.

***

The fun stops with a call from Liz the next morning. "Apparently they're dropping the charge against Nielle for Barney's death," she says.

"They're what? There's nothing on the news—"

"Tell me about it. Cops aren't talking, prosecutors aren't talking, Nielle's lawyer is spraying word salad like a chatbot on meth. WTF is going on?"

"Maybe it's just a rumor."

"This is from a court clerk who owed me a favor. And she's never let me down. If she says something is happening, it's happening. So, again, WTF?"

"I don't know," I say. "But I'll find out."

Avila doesn't pick up—not on the first try, the second, the third, or even the fourth. Nothing but dead air and a headache building behind my eyes.

So I drive to his office.

Public Safety headquarters is air-conditioned and quiet behind its tinted windows. I flash my ID at the front desk and say I need to see Lieutenant Avila. I get a bland smile and "he's in a meeting."

"Then I'll wait," I say, and plant myself in a plastic chair beside a fake ficus and sip from a lukewarm water bottle. Finally the receptionist buzzes me through.

Avila's office door is open, but he's looking out the window at the Marilyn statue like she might have hidden some answers under that billowing skirt. No treats on the credenza this time—he knows I'm stalking him.

I address his back. "Why are they dropping the charge against Nielle Lochner for her father's murder?"

He turns with a sigh—long and low, like a tire leaking air.

"I can't tell you," he says. "And you wouldn't believe me if I did. I can barely believe it myself and I saw it with my own eyes."

"Saw what?"

He pauses for a long time. "All I can say is, never in my entire life have I ever been more up to my eyeballs in shit than I am right now."

"What about Tony Alvarez? Is Nielle off the hook for his murder too? And Efren Mendoza? You're not saying she didn't do that one? It was her father's fucking gun, for fuck's sake!"

He sighs again. "Alvarez and Mendoza are county cases. They are Ray Jefferson's nightmare. All I can say is, stay tuned."

Ray Jefferson doesn't pick up either. I leave him a voicemail and crank up the Jeep for another trek to Thermal.

There, I get lucky. As I pull into the parking lot a little past noon, he's coming out the staff door, duty bag slung over one shoulder, key fob in hand.

I step out and walk over before he notices me. "How about some lunch? My treat."

He stops short. "Jesus, you trying to give me a heart attack? And no to lunch. I can't be seen with you right now."

"All right, then, let's do it here. The word is they're clearing Nielle Lochner of her father's murder."

He lets out a breath, slings his bag into the back seat of a black Chevy SUV, and gives a dry half-nod. "That's Avila's nightmare, thank God. I'm just glad it's not on my blotter."

I step closer. "That's what he said about your situation. So what about Tony Alvarez? He is on your blotter, because he was killed in Riviera Dunes, right? Has Nielle been cleared of that one too?"

He gives me a long look. "You're right, that one is my nightmare and Nielle has not been cleared. She is still charged with hiring Efren Mendoza to kill him."

"But if they're clearing her of Barney's murder, who do they think did it?"

He opens his car door. "I don't know. And if I did, I wouldn't tell you."

"And Efren Mendoza is on your blotter, too, right? You've still got Nielle for his murder, right? Or is that one unraveling too?"

He studies me. "So far it's holding. We think he came back for more money to leave the country because of all the heat after Barney's death, so she paid him, then killed him to shut him up. But I'd be lying if I said I'm a hundred percent sure of anything right now. You know how sometimes the deeper you dig, the weirder it gets? This is one of those times, but on steroids."

Then he steps into the Chevy and disappears down the lot.

After a few moments of thought, I text Jamie and ask for a meetup. "We need to talk. Something important."

She texts back "What is it?" and my phone chirps with an incoming pin drop.

I check the location and see she's at the La Paloma stables, where Barney's charity keeps its retired thoroughbreds. The horses there live better than most people. "I'll explain when I get there," I text back.

I find her in the East Paddock, a quiet corner of the property where tamarisk trees whisper in the wind and the only other sound is the distant hiss and whir of an irrigation system at the adjoining golf course.

Jamie's in riding gear, leading a gorgeous palomino mare around the paddock. The horse glides beside her like she owns the dirt. White mane brushed to a silken shine, golden coat glowing, rhinestone halter sparkling.

Jamie's doesn't see me until I'm leaning on the fence. She waves, completes her circuit, and stops in front of me.

"Meet Golden Girl," she says with a distant smile as she pats the horse's neck. "A wedding gift from Barney. So why are you here?"

"They're apparently dropping the charge against Nielle for Barney's murder."

"What?"

I say it again.

She sighs. "I knew it wasn't over." With an absent stare, she digs an apple out of the saddlebag and feeds it to Golden Girl. The horse switches her tail and nuzzles Jamie's shoulder.

"But how can they do that?" she says. "Skeeter obviously did it. You know she did."

"I don't know how they're doing it, but apparently they are. This is from a source who never misses."

"If they're letting her off the hook, that has to mean they'll charge me again, right? For Barney and Tony both, just like before, right? Because they were both killed with the same gun, my gun, and the same M.O., that's what you call it, right? And that drug dealer—do they think I killed him, too? I mean, I was at the Parsons then, but does that even matter now?"

"I don't know what they think and my source doesn't know either. The cops aren't talking, the lawyers aren't talking, nobody's talking. I'll set up a meeting with Ike. Look for a text."

Golden Girl flicks her ears and nickers. Jamie just stands there, hands on the pommel, staring out across the sand at the San Jacintos.

"This will never be over," she says softly, with fury. "Fuck."

It's the first time I've heard her swear.

An hour later, the two of us are at the Sand Trap Roadhouse, the only dive bar worthy of the name in a town where most people are too fancy for outlaw country from a juke box and beer that comes without a glass unless you ask for one.

We've set up shop at Ike's usual table in the back, far enough from the action for confidential talk if the place isn't too full.

Ike comes in and joins us. The barmaid, Rusty, brings a menu for Jamie, but doesn't bother for Ike and me. She knows we'll have the same as always: burgers and Bud.

Jamie orders white wine and arugula salad.

Rusty laughs and says, "As if. I'll bring the house salad."

When it comes, Jamie picks at it in silence. The jukebox blares Hank Williams Jr.'s "Family Tradition" too loud but no one complains. I lean in close so Ike will hear me over the din.

"What are they telling you?"

He shakes his head and reaches for the mustard. "Nothing. Calls to Public Safety and the DA go to voicemail or, hell, maybe Neptune. Wherever, you don't hear back."

Jamie lowers her fork and looks up, pale under the desert tan. "If they're dropping the charges against Skeeter, how does that not mean they'll circle back to me again? Not just for Barney but for Tony also and maybe this drug dealer, what, Martinez?"

"Mendoza." Ike taps the table for emphasis. "Efren Mendoza. But that's exactly what I'm afraid of. You have a dead rich guy and no arrest, you've got the city council and the visitors bureau both looking for somebody to fire and the cops looking for somebody to charge. Now if they would just return my fucking calls."

My last stop for the day is the wind farm on Indian Canyon Drive north of town. The moon is full and high, painting the whirling blades white and casting long, lazy shadows across the sand. A warm breeze off the alluvial fan sighs through the scrub. The Chaplain and I are leaning on the rear fender of his Harley.

"I heard the same rumor," he's telling me. "Nothing solid, but I found Mendoza's body. If Nielle walks on that one, too, who do you think they look at next?"

I don't have an answer. After a moment, I ask, "You want to come up to the house? Maybe stay over?"

He shakes his head, the moonlight picking out glints of silver in his beard. "Sorry, *cariño,* not tonight. I have to disappear for a while."

"Disappear? Where?'

"Mexico." He shrugs. "Till we find out who they're after if Nielle really does walk."

He kisses me and climbs onto the bike and kicks it to life. He nods once and pulls away across the sand toward Indian Canyon, lights off as usual.

Back home, I sit with Duke on the patio, mule in hand, admiring the moonlight.

"What now?" I ask myself. "If Efren and Nielle didn't kill Tony and Barney, who did?"

Imaginary Frank answers from the shadows.

"Who's left?" He's in an Adirondack chair a few feet from my table, Stetson on his knee, Partagas glowing in his hand.

"Nobody," I say. "Not as far as I can see."

He draws on the Partagas and lets the smoke out slow. "Why not Jamie?"

"But Jamie..." I falter to a stop when I realize how many times I've been through "why not Jamie?" in this case.

"Fuck if I know," I say.

"Same here," he says. "I only know what you know."

A coyote yips in the brush and Duke rockets off into the darkness. Frank flicks the Partagas into the sand, puts on his Stetson and jogs after him.

I'm ready to wrap up the day when my phone pings. It's face down on the arm of my chair, so I can't see who it is.

At first, I don't pick up, figuring the caller will keep trying if it's critical. If not, it'll keep till I'm in bed and making my last phone check of the day after I do the Wordle.

No such luck. It goes silent for about 30 seconds, then pings again. I tap it to life and put it to my ear without even checking the ID.

"You coming down or what?" Ernetta says. "You know how Louis is. He said he would give you case updates, and he won't stop till you get them. He's driving me crazy."

I'm about to launch another round of "second Tuesday" when it dawns on me that I'm stalled out on the Jamie Lochner case and everything touching it. I have no idea what to do next.

So, why not a trip to Slabs, with date shakes and maybe grilled rattlesnake outside Louis's tank? And, of course, Louis's updates, for what little they're apt to be worth? At least the trip will take my mind off the Lochner family.

"Yeah, sure," I tell Ernetta. "I'll be there tomorrow. It's supposed to hit 102, so maybe later in the day when weather's cooler? After his nap, okay?"

Ernetta muffles, then comes back after a few seconds. "Louis says he'll kill Molly for you and don't forget the shakes."

She taps off before I can ask who Molly is, so I open my laptop to finish the day with a news cruise.

A snowbird named Mimi Klein has posted a screen grab of tomorrow's 102-degree weather forecast. Underneath it, she shares a recipe for mailbox lasagna:

- Assemble lasagna in small 5x9 pan.

- Place lasagna in mailbox by 10am, leave 4-8 hours to cook.

- Return home, grab mail, grab dinner, enjoy your mailbox lasagna.

A commenter on the post is not optimistic: "Hope the mailman doesn't take it thinking it's a treat for him."

I close the laptop and finish my drink.

Chapter Twenty-Four

SO MUCH FOR COOL WEATHER later in the day. The dash in my Jeep says it's still 95 degrees when I pull out of Westmoreland with the date shakes for my rendezvous with Louis and Ernetta.

And inside the Jeep? Maybe 115 from being parked in the sun. As I crank up the AC, I worry about the sweat pooling under my arms. Then I remember, it's the Slabs. To live in the Slabs is to stink, because there's no air conditioning down there. Or plumbing. The bathing options are to take a dip in the nearby hot springs or shower with hauled-in water, which can run up to fifty bucks per fill-up for a standard 250-gallon tank.

Louis does not have a water tank and nobody goes to the hot springs when daytime highs are hitting 110 degrees, so I figure my level of fragrance is unlikely to exceed those of Louis and Ernetta. Lucky for Louis they have a shower at the Brawley sheriff's station. Otherwise he would be unemployably pungent for half the year.

As I pull up to his Faraday tank a little after seven, the blue women on the side of it are still riding the ocean depths on their giant sea beasts and the sun is kissing the crests of the Santa Rosas. Ernetta is lighting a propane lantern hung from a branch of their palo verde tree. She's in her standard uniform of shorts and t-shirt, but not the usual flip-flops. Tonight she's sporting a pair of neon green sneakers with bright red laces. A cigarette dangles from the corner of her mouth, the tip like a firefly in the gathering dusk.

As I swing down from the Jeep, I see she's already got the grill fired up.

"Dana, this is Molly right here," she tells me as she probes a sizzling chicken breast with a barbecue fork. "She was such a sweet little hen, laid the best eggs I ever ate. I told Louis, I says, 'Louis, don't you kill little Molly, you kill that Lydia, she'll taste just as good.' But he wouldn't do that, not Louis. He says, 'No, Miss Ernetta, Dana must have our best hen and that is Molly.'"

"Well, I'm truly grateful," I say. "To tell the truth, I'm not that fond of rattlesnake meat like we had last time anyway. It's tasty enough, but it just doesn't seem like anything a human being should eat."

"You can't eat rattlesnake eggs, though," Ernetta says.

This is a non sequitur of such epic proportions I immediately change the subject. "Is Louis up from his nap yet?"

"Oh, yeah," Ernetta says. "He's off in the bushes somewhere peeing, he'll be back directly. You bring the shakes?"

"Absolutely," I say. I go back to the Jeep, open the rear hatch, and haul the Coleman cooler over to the picnic table as the surviving hens cluck peacefully from Louis's coop.

While he is taking care of business, Ernetta catches me up on the latest gossip.

The new sneakers, she explains, are thanks to a Slabber named Luci Victus who's running her annual shoe drive. Ernetta shows me Luci's Facebook post on her phone. The photograph shows about a hundred pairs of donated shoes spread out on the sand with a note from Luci asking people to take no more than one pair. Underneath, a guy calling himself Markus Oralius comments that he's looking for "1 boot."

Which is bullshit, according to Ernetta. "I know that Markus," she says. "He's got two feet like the rest of us. That's the kind of joke gives the Slabs a bad name."

"Louis can't buy you new sneakers?" I ask. "He makes decent money at the sheriff's department."

"I don't know," Ernetta says. "He's been buying cryptocoins with it, I think he said."

"Louis is buying cryptocoins."

"Uh-huh. What is that?"

"Beats me," I say. "Pixie dust maybe?"

We share a laugh over that, then she moves on to the big news in the Slabs: The county sheriff's department saved a Slabber named Ollie a couple days earlier. This was when his German Shepherd, Nytro, jumped into the Coachella Canal at the north edge of the Slabs and couldn't get out. Ollie jumped in to save him but was also unable to get out. When he stopped trying and turned into a floater, somebody made an exception to the prime directive of life in the Slabs and called 911. A deputy sheriff who was on patrol a couple miles away responded, pulled Rollie out, applied chest compressions, and got him going again.

Equally important, according to Ernetta, was that the fire department showed up right after the deputy, and pulled Nytro out of the canal, too. Unlike his master, Nytro didn't require chest compressions.

"So when your Slabbers start down-mouthing the deputies, I stop 'em right there," Ernetta says. "Deputies are mostly decent people, like you were in your day."

Just then I sense a presence in the dusk and turn to see Louis making his way around the palo verde tree in ragged cargo shorts, an East Jesus sweatshirt with the sleeves hacked off, and what look like Ernetta's old flip-flops. His features, simultaneously familiar and strange, make me want to hug him as always: the fluffy build, the small, wide-set eyes and bowl-cut hair, the big uncertain smile.

But I just say "Hi." With Louis, hugging is a line you don't cross.

"Hello," he says without eye contact as he opens the cooler. He takes a date shake out of its ice nest and hands it to me, then one to Ernetta. The last one he keeps for himself as he settles onto a bench at the picnic table.

He takes a huge slurp, as do I. Then he gives me a sidelong glance, the closest he ever comes to eye contact.

"Dana, that is Molly that Miss Ernetta is cooking. Molly was my best hen. I saved her for you."

"Ernetta told me that, Louis. I'm very grateful."

"Dana, your gratitude is appropriate. I accept it."

We work on our shakes till Ernetta serves up the late Molly on a platter and disappears into the Faraday tank. In a moment, she's back with paper plates, plasticware, bottled water, and a can of baked beans she's already opened.

Louis finishes his plate first, and shoots Ernetta one of his sideways glances.

"You don't need to say it, Louis. I know I'm not LEO." She stands and takes her plate and water bottle into the tank.

"Dana," Louis says, "you are here for the updates."

I nod. "You are correct, Louis. Thank you for making the information available to me."

I'm not expecting much tonight, but I don't want to hurt Louis's feelings. Plus, I like date shakes and I like Louis. I even like Ernetta, because she takes care of Louis.

This time, Louis doesn't bring out his laptop. That means he's already gone over the updates and now they are stored forever in that strange brain of his.

"The first update is that a digital forensics consultant in San Jose sent an email to Lt. Avila at the Palm Springs Public Safety Department stating that the Lochner video is authentic, unedited, and not generated by an artificial intelligence, and that a full report will be forthcoming."

He punctuates this with a loud slurp of date shake.

"There's video?"

"Apparently," Louis says. "This email is the first reference to it in the records."

"But the email doesn't say what's on it?"

"No, Dana. I am sorry." He covers his mouth and belches.

"Can I see the information myself?"

Louis shoots me a sideways look that says I should know better than to ask. "I am sorry, Dana. You are not presently an LEO. You are only a former LEO. As such, you are not personally allowed to review any records. I will tell you any relevant information on a need-to-know basis."

"Sorry, Louis."

"Dana, you are forgiven. Do you wish information on the second update?"

"Please, Louis."

"It is in regard to Mr. Lochner's autopsy, Dana. According to the update, he was in the early stages of Creutzfeldt–Jakob Disease, possibly undiagnosed."

"Kroits-what?"

"Creutzfeldt-Jakob disease, Dana, also called CJD. It is a rare, incurable neurodegenerative disorder caused by misfolded proteins called prions. They trigger a chain reaction, causing folding of additional proteins and leading to brain damage and rapid cognitive decline."

"Wait a minute. Barney was dying?"

"Not immediately, as he was in the early stages of CJD. However, it is almost always fatal in the long run, with the familial form usually progressing more slowly."

"But he wasn't aware he had it?"

"Unknown, Dana, as noted in the update."

"Well, thanks. I guess. Are there additional updates?"

"No, Dana, there are not. But I will keep you apprised."

"Thank you, Louis. I am sure this information will prove useful."

"That is my hope, Dana."

I'm halfway back to Palm Springs when the bell that's been ringing in my head ever since Louis mentioned the "Lochner video" finally stops and produces the memory that's been trying to surface. The memory is what Avila said when he refused to tell me why Nielle was being cleared of killing her father: "I wouldn't believe it myself if I hadn't seen it."

I tap my phone to life and tell it to call Ike at home.

***

"THERE'S A VIDEO?" Ike says. "Christ, what next?"

It's the next morning and we're gathered in his office for yet another strategy session on the murder case that will not die, or even nap for more than ten seconds. I've just reported on my visit to the Slabs.

Ditto is asleep on Ike's desk blotter. Ike picks him up and sets him on the floor. He stalks to his box, settles in, and glares at me out of his one yellow eye. It makes me wish I had a crucifix to ward him off.

"So what's on the video?" Jamie asks. "Does it show who killed Barney? And how did they get my gun if it wasn't Skeeter? Could it be front gate video? Or doorbell video from the neighborhood? Did somebody sneak in?"

"Like I said, my source hasn't seen the video," I tell her. "All he saw is an email saying it's been authenticated and the full report is coming."

"Could it show you killing Barney?" Ike asks.

"No, Ike, it could not show that," Jamie says. "Because that did not happen. So stop asking me if it did. And if the video did show me doing it, I'd already be arrested again, right?"

"Probably." Ike begins flipping a pencil. "But let's remember, we don't even know for sure it actually clears Nielle, because they still haven't officially dropped the murder count against her for Barney's death. All we have at present is courthouse rumors and three words: 'the Lochner video'"

"Maybe they're waiting for the final report on it before they do anything," I suggest.

Ike nods. "That would be my guess."

"Well, I'm not waiting," Jamie says. "This crap has gone on long enough. Let's get the video and see for ourselves. Can't we file a motion?"

"We're not a party to this," Ike says. "Right now you're not charged with anything but the hit-and-run on the lady's car in Riviera Dunes."

Jamie tosses her head. "I don't care. I want to see that video."

"Look, you're asking me to file a motion on behalf of someone who's no longer a party to the case to get a video that we're not a hundred percent sure even exists, and may be irrelevant if it does. And our grounds is courthouse gossip that the prime suspect in the case is about to be cleared? Complete waste of time and money."

"It's my money," Jamie says. "I want you to do it."

Ike thinks it over. "Sorry, Jamie, but I just can't. It's legal nonsense. You can fire me if you want, but any reputable attorney will tell you the same thing."

"I don't care," Jamie says. "And you are fired. I'll find somebody else."

"Whoa, whoa, whoa," I say with a push of my hands. "Let's not rush into anything. Maybe there's another way forward here."

"What way?" Ike and Jamie say at the same time.

"When I asked Gary Avila why they were letting Nielle off, he wouldn't tell me anything. But he did say that I wouldn't believe it if he did tell me. And then he said, and I quote, "I can barely believe it myself and I saw it with my own eyes.""

"With his own eyes?" Ike says. "He said that?"

"He did."

"So there's obviously a video," Jamie says.

"And Avila's seen it," I say. "How about I take a run at him? He owes me."

"Dana, no," Ike says. "Let's not poke the bear."

"Why not?" I ask. "If he turns me down, we're no worse off than we are now. If he says 'yes,' then we'll finally find out what's going on, including if it's nothing."

"I guarantee you the answer will be 'no'," Ike says. Then he shrugs. "But I won't try to stop you."

Jamie looks at me. "What are we waiting for?"

Half an hour later, we're staked out in the Sand Trap parking lot in my Jeep. The engine's idling, the AC is straining against the 101-degree heat, and we've run through our pitch to Avila twice.

"What if he doesn't come?" Jamie asks.

"Then we'll ambush him at work. But he'll come. He always eats lunch here. Especially on Fridays."

Just then Avila rolls into the parking lot in his official police lieutenant rig, a black-and-white Ford SUV.

"Bingo," Jamie says. She opens her door and puts a foot on the asphalt.

"Nah, let's give him a few minutes," I say. "Once he gets his ribs and Corona, he'll be too committed to bail when he sees us."

When we walk in, Avila's on his regular stool at the bar, buried in his phone with a beer glass and a half-rack in front of him.

As planned, Jamie slides onto the stool to his right. "Hey, stranger, looking for a good time?"

Avila turns and says, "Buzz off or I'll—" He gapes for a moment at the apparition before him: a beautiful rich woman rather than the strung-out hooker he was expecting. "I'm off the clock. Go away."

By now, I've mounted the stool to his left. "A real cop is never off the clock, Gary."

He swivels to look at me. "Oh, fuck, you, too? What did I do to deserve this?"

"You made my life a living hell for absolutely no reason is what you did," Jamie says. "You turned me into a punchline. I'm Barney's Fatal Filly now."

"We proceeded on the basis of the evidence before us," he says.

"Except for when I said I didn't do it and you didn't believe me," Jamie says. "If Skeeter's being cleared of killing Barney, you're going to arrest me again, right?"

Avila gazes at her with a thoughtful frown. "Not if I have anything to say about it."

"What?" Jamie says. "So the video does clear me?"

"How the fuck do you know about—"

"Thanks for confirming it, Gary," I say. "Now show it to us."

"I'm not confirming anything but if there is a video, I can't show it to you."

"Remember when I gave you guys that slug from Barney's firing range and blew the case open? You said you owed me and now I'm here to collect. I won't leak it, just show us the damned video."

"What video?" He takes a swallow of Corona. "You've got all you're getting from me."

"Thanks, Gary." I jerk my head at Jamie and we head for the door.

"What did he mean, we've got all we're getting?" she says. "We got nothing, right?"

"Wrong. He confirmed there's a video and he told us you're off the hook because of it."

"I am?"

"When he said you won't be arrested if he has anything to say about? Trust me, he does."

Jamie's silent as we head back to Ike's office to pick up her Mercedes.

"What? You should be happy. You're officially off the hook. Or as officially as you can be till the D.A. actually dismisses the charges against Nielle for killing her father and releases the video."

"You sure they'll release it?"

"Well, of course they...huh."

"Huh what?"

"Maybe they don't have to. They could just say the charges are being dropped in the interest of justice and never release it."

"I still want to see it," Jamie says. "Or at least talk to somebody who did."

"Me too. But I just don't see how that's possible if the video's never admitted into evidence. You heard Ike. We don't have standing to—"

"Maybe Skeeter has seen it."

Chapter Twenty-Five

"LEAVE EVERYTHING but your ID in the car," I tell Jamie as we pull into the parking lot at the Palm Springs jail.

"Even my phone?"

"Even that. Otherwise they'll make you put it a locker."

We drop our bags and phones into the Jeep's console and present our IDs at the glassed-in reception window in the lobby. I make our request through the speaker grille to a sour-faced woman in a white police department polo. She makes a call to the back.

"Visitors for inmate Nielle Lochner," she says. "Dana Forsythe and Jameson Lochner." There's a pause, then "Sure."

"They'll let me know if the inmate will see you," she tells us through the scratchy speaker. "Wait over there."

She points to a row of plastic chairs in institutional blue bolted to the floor along the opposite wall.

"You really think Nielle will see us?" I ask Jamie when we're seated.

"She's the curious type. She did see us when we pulled up to her pool house, remember?"

"True. And it's not like she's got much else to do. But her lawyer probably told her not to talk to anybody."

"She wouldn't listen if he did. She's rich."

Now we're out of conversational fodder. Waiting these days is hard without a phone.

I fit myself to the hard blue plastic as well as possible and study the room, which smells like floor cleaner. Overhead, a fluorescent light fixture buzzes and flickers.

The waiting area is empty except for us and a middle-aged Latina. Her expression says she half expects to be locked up like whoever she's come to visit, either that or hauled away by Immigration. Our eyes meet, we nod, break gazes, and leave it at that.

On the beige cinderblock wall to my right is a bulletin board full of faded flyers, business cards from bail bondsmen, and signs warning "NO CELL PHONE" and "INMATES MAY REFUSE VISITORS."'

To my left, a wall-mounted TV plays *CNN en Español*. The audio is muted, but it's clear the story is about the latest mass shooting, this time at a children's hospital in Florida. I know enough Spanish to read the crawler at the bottom. It reports eight dead. One MD, two nurses, and "*cinco niños*"—five children.

The Latina goes to the reception window. I catch "*dos horas*" from her and "I'll check again" from the sour-faced woman as she picks up the phone.

"How long is this gonna take?" Jamie asks.

I point at the reception window. "She's been here *dos horas*."

Jamie frowns. "Two hours. Now I wish I had kept my phone until they put it in the locker."

At this point, I'm inclined to agree.

A guy comes in I recognize, though I can't place him at first. He's in flip-flops, cargo shorts, and a bleached-out Pride t-shirt.

Plus, he could use a shave and some time on the Peloton. He waits at the reception window until the Latina finishes, then steps up and greets Sour-Face by name. Maybe "Gina," but I'm not sure.

She beams and calls him Sammy and then I remember. He's Sammy Slater, a bail bondsman famous for bus-bench ads featuring his face, phone number, and slogan: OUT SOONER NOT LATER WITH SAMUEL J. SLATER.

He gives Sour-Face a name I don't catch, she nods and picks up her phone. He turns, and our eyes meet. Again, a brief nod suffices.

A few minutes later a door opens at the end of the lobby and an overweight corrections officer with a bad beard calls out "Maribel Nuñez?" The Latina hurries over and they disappear down a hallway.

Moments later, a blade-thin female corrections officer calls my name and escorts us down the same hallway, runs us through a metal detector, then takes us to the same visitation room where we interviewed Jamie about the hitman several days ago.

This time there's no conference table involved—that's for lawyer-client visits only. The officer points to a visitation booth—somewhat like two library carrels face to face—where we see Nielle already seated. She's behind a glass partition with an "ALL CALLS RECORDED" sign. No brown glasses today, orange jumpsuit, no makeup, unwashed hair hanging in greasy strands.

We take the two chairs on our side of the glass. I pull the intercom phone off its bracket and hold it between Jamie and me so we can both hear.

Nielle sits motionless and stares at us through the glass. Maybe a minute passes before she picks up the phone on her side.

"Thank you for seeing us," I say. "We—"

"Why are you here? And why did you bring the slut?"

"We heard they're dropping the charges you killed your father because of the video," I say. "We want to see it."

"You know about the video?"

"Does it show you shooting your father?" Jamie says.

"Shut up, slut," Nielle says. "You know I would never shoot my daddy."

"That's not what people are saying," Jamie says.

Nielle's face crumples and the ghost of a teenage girl looks out at us. "I...I...he...he...I would never shoot my daddy. But he...he...made me...he said Skeeter you have to do this...we have to do it...so that bitch...so she...they'll put her in jail...that bitch." She pushes the glasses up over her brows. Her eyes are red, swollen, and wet. She trains them on Jamie. "This is your fault, slut...if you could keep your knees, keep your knees..."

She collapses into snuffles and sobs, and pulls the glasses back down.

Jamie lowers the intercom phone between us, leans over, and whispers. "She's off her meds. We may not get anything—"

But Nielle is talking again. "If you could keep your knees together, slut, he...we would...he was so sick and you...you...they have it, my phone, I knew they would take it after you came to my house and said I...you said I killed my daddy... the police...you would tell the police and they...so I...the copy and Lolita ...it's all I have left of my daddy."

She pushes the glasses up and looks at me. "Can you get it...Lolita...if they...if the police take it...take it too if...I won't have him...have anything left of him that I...I wanted something...something..."

"Nielle, who is Lolita and what does she have?"

"She...she...Lolita...the copy."

"Sure," I say. "I can get the copy, Nielle. But who is Lolita?"

Jamie elbows me and whispers again. "Never mind, I know what she means. Just find out what Lolita has."

"Sure, Nielle," I say. "I'll get it from Lolita. What is it that she has?"

She looks around nervously, then whispers into her. "The jail if they play this recording...will they...they could tell the police..."

"Don't worry, they won't play this recording of us talking unless they think you're planning to break out of here. Now what does Lolita have?"

She whispers again. "On my phone, the video from...from...the video I made on my phone the police have...they have my phone but card—the card—" She stops and shakes her head. "And I so I—the card in my phone I...the video on the card...Lolita has it."

It takes me a few seconds to sort this out. "Nielle, are you saying the video is on a card from your phone, but the police don't have it?

"The phone," Nielle says. "They have it on my phone...but a copy – but my copy...Lolita she has it."

"So there's a copy of the video on a card from your phone? There was a memory card in your phone and you copied the original video to that and you hid the card so the police wouldn't get it?"

Nielle nods. "Lolita has...I gave...Lolita. Can you get it...and...and keep it...till I get...till they let me, I'm out...it, I made it...it's all I have."

"Sure," Jamie says. "I will, I promise. But where- -"

Too late. A corrections officer steps through the door behind Nielle and says. "Times up, Lochner. Let's go."

Nielle puts the phone mouthpiece to her lips and whispers "She...Lolita...she has it." Then she stands and the officer leads her away.

Back in the Jeep, the upholstery is like lava. I start the engine and crank the AC all the way up. The dash tells me it's 103 outside and it has to be twenty degrees hotter inside.

I turn to Jamie, who's hovering over the seat to keep the backs of her thighs off the upholstery.

"Serves you right for wearing that sundress," I don't say.

Instead I do say, "What the hell was that?"

"Like I said, Nielle must be off her meds." Jamie drops down on the seat to test the temperature, then resumes the hover. "Don't they give them meds in jail?"

"They're supposed to, but there's always screwups. I'll have Ike call her lawyer about it. But again, what the hell was that? Who's Lolita?"

"*Lolita* is her favorite book. Barney gave it to her. For her fifteenth birthday, I think she said." Jamie tries the seat again and this time stays put.

"What father gives his daughter *Lolita* on her fifteenth birthday?"

"Yeah."

"But that's where she hid the copy of the video?"

"Apparently."

"So where's the book?"

Jamie signals me "hang on" with a raised forefinger and closes her eyes in thought. "Um, I think, wait, I think she kept it in her room, no, wait, no, it was on the bookshelf in his study. Barney wanted it in his study."

"So it's in the mansion?"

"Yeah."

"Can we get in?"

"Sure. I moved back in once the police released it from being a crime scene."

"Seriously?"

"Why not? I own it. Or maybe only half of it if Nielle really is off the hook for killing Barney. Whatever, I'm living there. It's kind of a trophy."

Twenty minutes later, we're in Barney's study with our hands on our hips and frustrated expressions on our faces. That's because *Lolita* does not appear on the bookshelf in the study.

Also missing, Jamie says, is the leather-upholstered armchair that once stood behind Barney's huge mahogany desk. "The police took it and never brought it back. Maybe Ike can get it for me?"

"Another trophy?"

"The ultimate trophy. Barney was killed in that chair."

"Okay. But back to business. What about *Lolita*? Maybe in Nielle's room?"

Jamie shudders. "I was only in there once, when she showed me the book. I'm never going in that room again."

"Why?"

"You'll see."

She leads me upstairs to Nielle's bedroom. It's next to the master bedroom. Daddy's bedroom.

She opens the door for me, then steps back. I step in.

Morning sun filters through gauzy curtains in a pale blush tone. The pillows on the bed are fluffed, the covers turned down as if waiting for Nielle to return.

There's a sense of arrested development about the space. The furniture is grown-up—sleek white lacquer, plush headboard, a walk-in closet with mirrored doors. But the vibe is stuck somewhere between little girl and prom queen.

Photos line the dresser. Nielle and Barney at various ages. A teenage Nielle on horseback, Barney holding the reins and beaming. A twenty-something Nielle at a charity gala in a strapless dress, Barney's hand at her back.

Over the bed, a big photo of her as a girl of nine or so, barefoot in a sundress in a field of flowers, gazing adoringly at the unseen photographer.

There's a jewelry tray full of dainty chains and heart-shaped pendants. A pair of sandals lies under the vanity chair like she had just kicked them off when Barney exiled her to the pool house.

And on the nightstand: a hardcover copy of *Lolita*.

I pick it up, flip it open, and read the inscription aloud. "To my cinnamon girl, the light of my life. —D"

I turn to Jamie, who's watching from the doorway. "Did you ever read this book?"

"I couldn't make myself touch it after I saw the inscription."

"Well, that language is straight out of the book. Cinnamon girl? The light of his life? Those were the pervert's nicknames for Lolita. Just how close were these two?"

"It was probably what it looks like," she says. "But I never knew how for sure. Didn't want to, still don't."

"Well, let's do this." I drop onto the bed and start to riffle through the pages.

"I'm not coming in there," Jamie says.

"Oh, sorry, yeah. So downstairs or—"

"My dressing room," she says. "Follow me."

She crosses in front of the master bedroom and stops at a set of double doors on the other side of it.

"Nielle on one side, you on the other, Daddy in the middle," I say. "No wonder you wanted her out of the house at night."

"No way was I having her in the next room when we...you know." She shudders and swings the doors open and I give a low whistle. What I'm looking at is like a luxury hotel suite—creamy suede walls, polished floors, and mirrors on every surface. It smells of citrus, perfume, and fuck-you money. Through an open doorway, I catch a glimpse of the bathroom. Floor of pale stone and a freestanding tub shaped like a teardrop parked under a huge frosted window.

"You call this a dressing room?"

Jamie flashes that familiar little cynical smirk, the one that says she knows how ridiculous this all is, but still. "Exactly," she says.

We pull velvet stools up to the vanity and I open *Lolita* again. Riffling the pages doesn't pay off, not the first time, or the time after that. I turn the book so it opens downward and riffle the pages two more times. Still nothing.

I pull off the dust jacket and shake that, too. Nothing but the dry papery scent of old secrets.

"Maybe in the spine," Jamie says.

"Yeah, same thought." I run a thumb down it. A couple inches from the top, I feel a tiny square bump. Maybe.

"We need something sharp," I say.

Jamie opens a drawer in the vanity and comes up with a gold-handled nail file.

"Yeah." I wedge the point between the cloth cover and the spine and slice downward, peeling the strip of cloth back like a flap of skin.

Something drops out and bounces off the vanity with a tiny, high-pitched "tick." A Micro SD card, no bigger than a baby's fingernail.

We both stare at it in silence. Then Jamie speaks. "Suddenly it seems real."

"How do we watch it?" I ask. "Put it in one of our phones?"

"Hold on a second." Jamie heads for the desk in a corner of the room. It's modern and low-slung, lacquered white, the kind of thing that shouldn't have drawers but somehow does.

She pulls open the center one—a shallow, neatly organized tray lined with gray felt. Inside: three styluses, a Montblanc pen, a velvet pouch with adapter cables poking out the top, and a small zippered case that could hold either a fortune in loose diamonds or Jamie's collection of memory cards.

She fishes out a sleek metal hub the size of a stick of gum and holds it up. "Multi-adapter," she says. "You just stick the card in this slot here, then plug the whole thing into the iPad."

She gets the iPad off the nightstand, returns, inserts card into adapter and adapter into iPad, then brings the iPad to life and taps the Files icon. A grid of icons pops up. One of the icons—a video icon—is labeled "Daddy."

Neither of us speaks at first. We just stare. Finally I say, "Well?"

Jamie taps the icon. Up comes a preview image from the video, with a triangle you tap to play it. The preview image shows Barney's study. It's just like I saw it downstairs except that the big leather armchair he died in is in place behind the mahogany desk.

Jamie's lips part, just slightly. "Looks like we're in." She taps the dart.

Chapter Twenty-Six

THE SCREEN FLICKERS, then steadies.

We're in Barney's study, staring at his desk and chair. The view is waist-level. Nielle's phone must be set up on the globe bar at the side of the room.

Her voice comes first, offscreen, high and pleading. "Daddy, please. Just let me do this one thing."

"Skeeter, no. Turn it off. This is hard enough without—"

"I need it, Daddy. I need to have something left of you."

Barney steps into the frame from the right, walks to his desk, and drops into the chair. He's in a blue oxford, sleeves rolled up, no tie. The liver-spotted hands are gloved in black nitrile. He looks tired and resigned.

"It's a bad idea, baby. If anyone finds it—"

"They won't. I'll hide it. I promise." Her voice cracks. "Please, Daddy. Just let me have this one last thing."

A long pause. Barney rubs his temple with one gloved hand.

"All right," he says at last. "All right, if it means that much to you. But you hide it good, you understand? We can't have the cops find it."

"I understand. Thank you, Daddy."

The picture jiggles, presumably from Nielle checking the phone. Then she walks into the frame from the left, back to the camera. She's wearing jeans, a sweatshirt, and nitrile gloves.

"Okay, Daddy, it's on, but we could find another specialist. The one in LA, he wasn't—"

"I have CJD," he says. "I'm dying and we both know what's coming. I lose my mind, my body, everything. Look at this."

Barney raises one hand and holds it in front of his eyes. The fingers twitch first, a quick, snapping tremor like a hiccup in the nerves. Then the whole hand jerks as if yanked by an invisible string. His brow furrows, as if he's willing it to hold steady, but the tremor comes again. His eyes stay locked on it with the baffled intensity of a man watching a piece of himself take on independent life.

"That's myoclonus." He shakes his head and lowers the hand. "Pretty soon I'll be unable to walk. I'll be pissing myself. Well, fuck that. I'm going out my own way while I still can. And I want that ungrateful little whore locked up for the rest of her life."

"Please, Daddy. Let's just have the Mexican kill her, too."

"No. I want her alive and thinking about how I beat her while she rots in prison. I want her wondering how the fuck I had that boyfriend of hers killed and then somehow did this today and stuck her with two counts of murder."

Barney pulls something from a drawer in his desk and lays it on the desk blotter. It's Jamie's little Ruger. "You know what to do after, right?"

"Yes, Daddy." Her voice is barely a whisper.

"You hide that phone and dump the gloves and bury that gun, right? And then you go out for bagels, same as always, right?"

"Yes, Daddy."

"Good girl. Now come give your old man a hug."

She goes to him and he pulls her in, strokes her hair like he's tucking her into bed.

"You love me more than her," she murmurs. "Right, Daddy?"

"Of course," he says. "You know you'll always be my cinnamon girl."

She sobs into his neck.

"Now you step back," he says. "We don't have much time. The whore just left and I have to die within a few minutes of that or the forensics might trip us up on the time of death. Like on *CSI*, right?"

Nielle nods, sobs, and steps out of the frame as Barney picks the Ruger up from the blotter. He tries to hold it steady but his hand starts to tremor. The gun wavers, dips. He grips it tighter, trying to force it still, but the shaking gets worse. A quick spasm jerks his whole arm.

"Goddamn it," he mutters. He sets the gun back on the blotter and flexes his fingers. He lifts the gun again, with both hands this time. The tremor is still there but it's better controlled. He turns his head to the left, presses the muzzle to his temple and closes his eyes.

"Love ya, baby. Don't forget where to bury this."

"Daddy, please—"

The Ruger cracks. Barney's head jerks sideways. He slumps back in the chair. His gun arm falls to his side, out of sight behind the desk.

The phone camera doesn't pick up a clear view of the wound in his temple, so it's not clear how much it's bleeding. But usually you don't get more than a trickle in cases like this. Nor is it clear if there's an exit wound. But probably not with a low-velocity weapon like a .22.

Nielle steps into the frame, stands in front of the desk, and stares at Barney for several seconds in silence. Then she walks around the end of the desk, picks the gun up from the floor, returns to the front of the desk, and fires twice into Barney's chest. The blue oxford jerks a little with each shot, dimpling and tearing as if poked with a stick. Red seeps outward from the two dark spots like spilled ink.

She slides the Ruger into a hip pocket and walks behind the desk. She peels the gloves from Barney's hands, then hers, then wads them together and stuffs them into her other hip pocket.

She bends and kisses the top of his head. "Love you, too, Daddy."

Then she walks toward us and vanishes to the left. The screen blurs pink as her hand covers the phone's camera lens. Then the video stops.

Jamie lets out a breath like she's been punched. Her arms are wrapped around herself.

I sit there, brain spinning.

CJD. Creutzfeldt-Jakob disease. Just like Louis said in the Slabs. I heard it. I even put it in my notes when I got home. But did I listen? No.

And because of that, I didn't see this coming.

"Jesus," Jamie says at last. "That poor girl."

Chapter Twenty-Seven

CINCO DE MAYO AT THE SAND TRAP, with a mariachi band loud enough to rattle the ice in my Moscow mule. But the place itself is close to deserted.

Early May in Palm Springs will do that. The temperature breaks a hundred most days now and will keep it up till September. The snowbirds have migrated north again, to places with lawns, summer showers, and towering shade trees instead of scrubby mesquite bushes clinging to life in the desert sand. What's left in Palm Springs are us locals gutting out the inferno that passes for summer in the Coachella Valley.

Liz, Lita, and I are at a corner table—me with my mule, Liz with her Corona longneck, Lita with her glass of chardonnay.

"So, Dana," Liz is saying. "Clear up one detail for me. How did this guy Mendoza get himself hired by Barney to kill Tony Alvarez if Tony originally hired him to kill Barney?"

"According to Ray Jefferson, my county mountie pal, the theory is that when Mendoza realized how rich Barney actually was, he figured, why work for a convenience store clerk in Riviera Dunes? And he had a cousin on the landscaping crew that serviced Barney's place, so, next thing you know, he's playing *Let's Make A Deal* with Barney and Nielle."

"Can't fault him on ambition, I guess," Liz says. "To the late Efren Mendoza." She raises her Longneck for a toast, and we all clink glasses.

She sets down her longneck and gives me the eye. "So what's the latest with your midnight biker?"

"Back from Mexico tonight, or so he says. Fingers crossed, it's been a while since my eyes rolled back in my head."

Liz laughs out loud. A couple drinks in and we both get raunchy.

Lita, not so much. "Dana!" she says with her usual frown of envy and disapproval.

"With any luck," I go on, "he'll be my ride home."

Liz raises her eyebrows. "Define 'ride.'"

I grin. "Exactly."

The laughter's still rolling when Jamie breezes in, sporting jeans and high-heel black cowgirl boots that shout just-bought. She props one on a chair and says, "Tony Lama. Eat your hearts out, ladies."

Liz whistles. "Well, hello, Dallas."

I shake my head. "What happened to Jimmy Choo?"

Jamie smirks. "You ride with a cowboy, you wear the boots."

"Cowboy?" Lita asks. "What cowboy?"

"Darren." Jamie drops into a chair and nods at the double rear doors of the Sand Trap. "He's out back now parking his truck."

"You own a Mercedes and an Escalade," I say. "And you're riding around in a pickup?"

"If you ever rode with a cowboy, you'd understand."

As if on cue the rear doors swing open and in he comes—pure Texas. Levi's that could stand unassisted, boots scuffed from real work, pearl-snap shirt tucked in neat, a Stetson tipped low. Shoulders built on hay bales, not gym weights, a grin of pure mischief.

"Howdy, ladies," he says.

Cornball, sure, and probably an act. But he pulls it off. Liz beams, and even I feel a little flutter. The hat and shoulders remind me of Frank.

Liz leans forward with a slow smile, hand out. "I'm Liz."

Darren takes it, grins, and says, "Howdy, ma'am. Jamie said I'd be meeting her friends tonight. She didn't say I'd be sitting at a tableful of desert roses."

Jamie shoots him a look. "Whoa back, there, cowpoke."

He chuckles and heads to the bar.

Jamie watches him go, then swings on Liz with a glare sharp enough to cut glass. "Back off, cougar. He's not on the menu."

Liz raises her hands in mock innocence. "Just checking out the dessert tray."

"Do it from a distance," Jamie snaps. "Anyway, I'm buying the stables where I board Golden Girl and Darren's gonna run it for me, plus manage Barney's thoroughbreds. We didn't make the Derby this year, obviously. But maybe next year."

I grin. "Maybe you can wrangle horses, Jamie, but can you really wrangle that cowboy?"

"I know, I know, he's all 'aw, shucks, ma'am,' at first. But then you find out he's got way more sense than he lets on."

"Wait a minute," Lita says. "It's less than a month since Tony was killed and you're already ...are you sure you—"

"Lita's right," I say. "Are you in your right mind enough for a decision this big?

Jamie's silent for a long time. "I hear you. But I only met two men in my life who made me feel like Tony and Darren did. Now one's dead and the other one, if I don't pull him into my life now, who knows where both of us will be tomorrow? I'm done with waiting."

Now I'm silent for a long time. "Actually," I tell her, "I know what you mean."

She says, 'Thanks," and tears up a little. After a moment, she brushes away the tears and leans in.

"Ike tells me Skeeter's lawyer wants me to testify to what I saw going on between her and Barney at the mansion," she says in a low voice. "He's trying to spin a story about Barney abusing her—emotional coercion, dependency, mental illness. He wants her to plead insanity."

"Is she gonna do it?" I ask.

"Not according to Ike. She just keeps saying, 'My Daddy would never do that.'"

"That's our Nielle," I say. "But are you gonna testify?"

"I don't know, maybe, after that video." She sighs. "I feel sorry for her."

"The same video where she wanted to have you killed, too?"

Jamie grimaces. "Sure, yeah, I hate her. It's just that—watching it, you almost forget how twisted she is. Almost."

"Accomplice to murder for helping Barney hire Efren Mendoza to kill Tony Alvarez," I remind her. "And murder one for killing Efren to shut him up."

She nods, and watches as Darren heads back from the bar with two Lone Stars.

"What did you decide to do with the video?" I ask.

"The police don't want it," she says. "They have the original. So I put it back where we found it."

"In *Lolita*? Seriously?"

She shrugs again. "I promised Nielle I'd keep it for her, so I guess I will. Until I can finally let go of all this."

Darren arrives with the sweat-beaded Lone Stars. They lift and clink, Darren says, "Here's to Palm Springs" and they drink. The rest of us repeat it and drink, too. Jamie and Darren head for the dance floor.

I notice Lita isn't saying much. She's just turning her wineglass on the table.

"You're quiet tonight, my friend," I say. "Everything all right?"

She exhales. "Mom's been gone two weeks now. The twins and I are hanging in, but somebody has to keep them steady. And with fall coming..."

She looks at me and lets it float in the air. Fall coming, as in Stanford, marriage, her own life out there waiting.

"It's time for you and Duke to move in with us," she goes on. "You're spending half your nights down here anyway. The kids would feel more settled and they adore Duke. And he adores them. They couldn't have a better protector than that dog."

I picture him asleep on their bed, or pacing the yard with them. The thought of trading my empty hilltop for that warmth and laughter tilts something inside me. My life bending toward theirs, whether I like it or not.

"And you have time now that Jamie's case is finally over," Lita goes on.

That something inside me has decided while I wasn't thinking about it. "Yeah, I'll start moving my stuff in the morning."

Lita beams and says, "*Gracias*, Dana. *Gracias*"

Liz smirks. "So you do have a nurturing instinct."

I sip from my mule. "Apparently."

The mariachi band belts out another chorus of *Cielito Lindo*.

Liz clinks her Corona against my copper mug. "But really, Dana. How did you do it? You cracked Jamie's case wide open like one of these things." She holds up a peanut-in-shell from the bowl on the table, cracks it and tosses the nuts into her mouth. "Without you she could still be looking at life in prison."

"Yeah, but I did miss Barney's Creutzfeldt-Jakob Disease. I still can't believe I let that slide after Louis told me about it. I could have tied the whole thing up a lot quicker and cleaner."

Liz elbows me. "So you missed one detail. You got there is what matters. You'll be fine."

I raise my mug. "A couple more of these and I will. Order me a refill, will ya?"

She raises a hand, waves it at the bar, then points down at me and nods. "Coming right up," she tells me. The band plays on, glasses clink, voices rise, people laugh. Jamie and Darren finish their dance, return to the table, and drink from their Lone Stars.

My phone buzzes. A text from a strange number pops up: *Outside.*

I push back my chair. "Never mind the refill. My ride's here."

"Define 'ride,'" Liz says again.

I grin. "Exactly."

They rib me some more as I gather my things, but I wave them off and push through the rear doors into the desert night. The lot's half empty and there's no Harley in sight. I peer around until I see the flash of a single headlight, then hear the Chaplain's engine cough to life.

***

An hour later, my bedroom smells of sweat, leather and Partagas smoke. My hair is damp curls on my neck. My right cheek stings from a beard burn.

"Nice to have you back," I say. "Been a while."

He exhales toward the ceiling. "*El sexo,*" he says, followed by too much rapid Spanish for me to catch.

"Translation?"

He grins through the beard. "Sex is God's apology for the rest of it."

"He owes us at least that much."

He slides an arm under my neck and kisses my cheek. We cuddle like that for a few minutes.

"That video you and Jamie found really blew things up, *sí?*"

I have to chuckle. "Especially after Liz put it online."

"Even in Mexico my relatives were talking about it. The crazy Palm Springs *gringa* lady with the big glasses and the little gun."

I pull the sheet higher. "Yolanda's in Mexico now and I'm moving down there tomorrow to look after the twins."

Silence from the other side of the bed.

"You could come in from the shadows like we talked about and live up at my place while I'm down here with the twins. Ike says he's making progress on getting your record expunged."

He's quiet for a long time. "I've been thinking about it. But after so long I wonder if I like the shadows too much now."

"I can wait," I say.

He brushes a strand of hair from my eyes. "*Gracias, cariño.*"

"But not forever."

He lies back, stubs out the Partagas in the ashtray on the nightstand, and rolls me over on top of him.

"I know."

The End

Continue the Series

If you'd like to see how Dana's story began, here's the first chapter of The Sand Garden —her debut case in Palm Springs.

She is still grieving from the shock of Frank's death on duty when she gets an even bigger shock: She learns he had twins with a secret mistress who's just been murdered.

Then the orphaned infants are dropped off on her patio in the middle of the night and she's hired to help defend the accused killer in the glittering desert oasis of Palm Springs.

Will she nail the real killer or become the next victim?

"Abandoned orphans, an outlaw biker, a murdered mistress--it's Dickens in the desert." -- RICH CHIAPPONE, author of THE HUNGER OF CROWS

THE SAND GARDEN

Copyright 2025
Stan Jones

CHAPTER ONE

THE CHAPLAIN comes by night.

He can't afford to be seen near anybody with law-enforcement ties. Not even an ex-cop and a cop's widow like myself.

If he was spotted at my place, his fellow Mogul bikers would plant him in the sand garden known as the Coachella Valley before the next sunrise painted the ocotillos yellow and orange.

So, the Chaplain comes by night.

This time, my clock radio reads 2:18 a.m. when I wake to hear his Harley mutter to a stop behind the house. My place is in the Cahuilla foothills of the San Jacinto Mountains overlooking Chapel City, Rancho Mirage, and—if you squint hard enough—the south end of Palm Springs.

It's remote enough that I can afford my house, which is critical since Frank, my husband, got himself killed on what should have been a routine domestic violence call and left me nearly broke. All I got was a mortgage in default, a zero balance in his 401K, and no explanation of where the money went.

Lucky for me California takes care of the widow when a cop gets shot in the line of duty. Eventually there was a death benefit that paid off the mortgage, and I get half of Frank's salary for the rest of my life.

But the 401K? Damned if I know what happened to it. He closed it with a cashier's check and there the trail ends. Someday I'll investigate and figure it out. But not yet. I can't make myself do it.

Oh, yeah, I almost forgot: Frank did leave me the Chaplain.

The Chaplain was Frank's confidential informant and he asked the Chaplain to look out for me if the worst happened to him.

Eight months ago, the worst did. A few nights after the funeral, the Chaplain showed up at my back door and told me the deal. Now he's my confidential informant, witness retriever, and secret go-to for things best done in the dark.

I peer out the window beside my bed, and I can see in the moonlight that the Chaplain has a sidecar on his Harley, and luggage carriers on the back. He's lifting something out of the sidecar.

A few moments pass and I hear stuff being set on the patio, followed by silence. Then he cranks up the Harley and vanishes into the night.

This is my arrangement with the Chaplain. I ask him to find something—most often an uncooperative witness—and bring him in. One time he explained to me how he does it.

The Chaplain's wanted, so he doesn't carry a gun unless he expects to need it, just a ball peen hammer. If a guy's uncooperative, the Chaplain will show him the hammer, give him a look, and wait.

The Chaplain is six and a half feet and two-hundred-plus pounds of beard, muscle, and biker menace, and who's to know what else is under those leathers? The guy usually becomes very cooperative, because the people I ask the Chaplain to track down are too deep into drugs, depravity, or gambling debt to go to the cops.

And when one doesn't cooperate, the Chaplain slams the hammer down on the table, drags the guy's hand out over the dent, raises the hammer, gives him another look, and waits some more. So far, that's always done the trick.

Except tonight there's a problem. The Chaplain's not working on anything for me at the moment, so what's he dropping off on my patio? I slide on my robe and slippers, and I'm halfway to the back door when my phone chimes from the nightstand.

I go back and pick it up. The caller ID shows the number for the Chaplain's current burner phone. It's always a burner with the Chaplain and he gets a new one every few weeks, then smashes the old one with his hammer and buries it in the desert. There's gotta be dozens of his old burners out there in the sand. Do the metal-detector people ever find them and wonder how they got there?

"What's happening?" I ask. "We've got nothing going on right—"

"Look on the patio. And stay on the line."

"But what—"

"Please, Dana."

The Chaplain's like that. Gracious but implacable.

I walk out of the bedroom trailed by Duke, my retired German Shepherd K-9 partner, and swing open the back door. The Chaplain has switched on the patio light before leaving, and it takes me at least thirty seconds to process what I see: twin toddlers, one of each flavor, two or three years old, asleep in car seats. Around them is a bunch of kid stuff in reusable shopping bags--clothes, diapers, toys, plastic kiddie cups and bowls, books with covers in bright colors. "Grumpy Bird" and "Emily's Balloon" are two that I can see. On their laps are a bedraggled stuffed pony and a one-eyed teddy bear.

"Jesus," I say into the phone. "What the hell is this?"

The Chaplain, for once, doesn't seem to know how to say what's on his mind. The seconds drag past.

"They're Frank's," he says finally. "Their mother was killed tonight. I didn't know what else to do with them."

I drop into a wicker chair, set my phone on the arm, pick it up, set it down again.

I study the kids in the car seats. The girl's a redhead, the boy has hair that reminds me of Frank. His hair was a beautiful black till it got streaked with gray, which only made him more beautiful. And the boy has Frank's nose and eyebrows, too. Duke sniffs his wrist and he wakes up. He peers around the patio, looks up at me with a sleepy half-smile, murmurs "Dukie." Duke licks his face and he falls back asleep.

The boy's smile nails it. Slightly crooked at the right corner, just like Frank's. Plus, he and Duke know each other. Frank must have taken Duke along when he was with his twins and their mother, the bastard.

"Dana?" the Chaplain says.

I go back inside and tap the phone onto speaker. "They're Frank's? My husband had kids with another woman?"

The Chaplain is smart enough to know when a man should keep his mouth shut.

I process for another while.

The Chaplain clears his throat and waits.

"What am I supposed to do with them?" I ask finally.

"I thought you'd know. Because you're..."

"Because I'm a woman, right? I'm a woman who couldn't have kids!"

More tactical silence from the Chaplain.

I sigh. "All right, I'll keep them till morning, then get hold of Child Protective Services. What are their names?"

"Rose and Sonny Williamson."

"Sonny?"

"Dana, I am so sor—"

"Frank. She named him Frank Junior. Didn't she?"

Another silence. I figure the Chaplain's debating if he can get away with saying nothing this time. Apparently, he decides not.

"Again, I am so sorry."

"Who was the mother? It's not another cop, is it? If it is, I swear, I'd kill her myself if she wasn't already dead. And how did she die? And how did you get those kids?"

"She was Jennifer Williamson. She was not a cop," the Chaplain says. "But the rest is too much to tell right now. You deal with the kids. You get some sleep. You put up the signal when you're ready. Then we'll talk."

"No, dammit, we'll talk now. Who was this bitch?"

But he's gone. I fight off the urge to call him back. He's told me never to do that. I tried, once. He blocked the call, buried the burner in the desert, and got a new one.

You don't call the Chaplain. He calls you.

TO LEARN MORE about The Sand Garden on Amazon, use the QR code or Internet link shown below:

https://a.co/d/51XgSa5

(Note: This link is case-sensitive. Use the uppercase X and S, as shown.)

www.ingramcontent.com/pod-product-compliance
Lightning Source LLC
LaVergne TN
LVHW041918070526
838199LV00051BA/2659